Mary Lee was so cold, so frozen, she might actually have been on a mountain, surrounded by snow.

Why had Madrigal come to visit? After saying over and over again that she had better things to do, why had Madrigal changed her mind and decided to come to the boarding school? She had not had Mother or Father's permission. She'd arranged it herself. Used the credit cards and gone. Mary Lee thought that was so neat when Madrigal told her: you wonderful, brave, good dear-sister, Mary Lee had thought! Yes! Coming to see your twin no matter what blockades are thrown in your way. True love!

But had it been ... true hate?

Classic Point Horror never dies...

Point Horror

TWINS

CAROLINE B. COONEY

■ SCHOLASTIC

Scholastic Children's Books,
Commonwealth House, 1-19 New Oxford Street,
London WC1A 1NU, UK
A division of Scholastic Ltd
London ~ New York ~ Toronto ~ Sydney ~ Auckland
Mexico City ~ New Delhi ~ Hong Kong

First published in the US by Scholastic Inc., 1994
First published in the UK by Scholastic Ltd, 1995

This edition published by Scholastic Ltd, 2000

Text copyright © Caroline B. Cooney, 1994

ISBN 0 439 01316 X

Printed by Cox and Wyman Ltd, Reading, Berks.

1 2 3 4 5 6 7 8 9 10

The right of Caroline B. Cooney to be identified as the author of this
work has been asserted by her in accordance with the Copyright,
Designs and Patents Act, 1988.

Chapter 1

They were sending Mary Lee to boarding school. She could not believe it. Identical twins — *separated*?

Mary Lee's lovely olive skin was stretched with fear. Her beautiful hazel eyes, with their fringe of long black lashes, were wide with panic.

Each swing of hair, each lift of brow, was mirrored in her identical twin. If it had been a fairy tale, and one twin had said, "Mirror, Mirror on the Wall, Who Is the Fairest of Them All?" the mirror could have made no answer. For *two* qualified.

"Listen," said Mary Lee, striving to stay calm. Her parents admired calm. "Madrigal and I have never been separated! You don't understand because you're ordinary people. But we're identical twins. We're not regular sisters. If you send one of us away, we won't be whole!"

"Nevertheless," said her mother, looking sad but sure of herself, "you are going."

Mother, who adored having identical twins, who loved dressing them just the same, and fixing their hair just the same, and admiring them in their perfect synchrony, now wanted them split up?

Mary Lee was shaking. There was no need to look at her twin, because whatever one did, the other did. Madrigal would also be shaking. One of the oddities of identical twins was that the girls themselves could never tell who started anything. Madrigal might well have started trembling first, and Mary Lee second. One of them was always the echo of the other.

There was no possibility of remaining calm. Frantic, Mary Lee cried, "Mother, you can't do this to us!"

Her parents were strangely still, perhaps braced against her screaming, perhaps rehearsed for it, dreading the moment when Madrigal, too, began screaming.

"We have given it a great deal of thought, sweetheart," said her father quietly, "and this is the right thing to do."

"You've spent seventeen years making us match!" shrieked Mary Lee. "And you pulled it off! Nobody can tell us apart. We are one. Now what has brought this on? What set you off? How can you possibly think separation is the right thing to do to us?"

Both girls were there, of course, because where one twin was, the other always was, too. And, yet, Mother and Father seemed to be talking only to Mary Lee. As if Mary Lee had come undone. As if Mary Lee needed to be repaired. As if boarding school were the solution to Mary Lee.

Sadly, her mother stroked Mary Lee's heavy black hair. Loosely caught behind her head in a cluster of bright yellow ribbons, the hair slid free and weighted down her shoulders. Mother's eyes were bright with unshed tears, and her heart was racing with sorrow.

Mary Lee could not imagine what was going on. Separation could only break the hearts of all four of them.

"Try to understand," said her mother brokenly.

But Mary Lee had no use for that instruction. "What is there to understand? You are ripping us away from our own selves!"

"Listen to your phrasing, Mary Lee. Madrigal is not *your* self," said Mother. "She is *her* self. We have allowed ourselves and the world to treat you as a unit. We were wrong. You are not one. You are two."

She and Madrigal were not run-of-the-mill sisters. Mary Lee could not imagine being shipped away like a package, wrapped in brown paper, tied with string. Waking up in the morning without her twin. Dressing without her twin. Going to class without —

It was unthinkable. She would not do it. "You brought identical twins into the world. You must accept what we are! We are one."

Mother was suddenly harsh and angry. "Mary Lee, listen to yourself. You say 'we' instead of 'I.' You say 'us' instead of 'me.' It isn't healthy. You need to be a girl named Mary Lee, not half a twinset. You must fly alone. Sing solo."

Mary Lee had never heard such a horrible idea. *Fly alone? Sing solo?* "Identical twins can't do that. You're fighting a biological fact."

"The fact," said Father, "is that we have decided to separate you and your sister. You will simply have to trust us that this is a necessary action. For your mental health and Madrigal's. Madrigal will stay home under our supervision. You will go to boarding school."

The house seemed to float around Mary Lee as if its rooms had fallen apart like badly stacked toy blocks. She turned to her sister, knowing that the force of her own turn would turn Madrigal as well. They did not imitate each other so much as simultaneously broadcast. They never knew which of them was first and which the follower. It was too quick for that. "We won't let them, will we, Madrigal?"

Her twin sister smiled. A smile Mary Lee did not share at all.

Her twin sister said, "I think it's a good idea."

One thousand nine hundred and twelve miles to the school.

On the big featureless airplane, in a gray sky, with a gray heart, Mary Lee felt each of the those miles pulse through her. One thousand nine hundred and twelve spaces between Mary Lee and her twin.

How can I do this? she thought, sick with fear. In my whole life I've never entered a room or a building without Madrigal.

This was not quite true. But she could count the exceptions.

There was the first week of fifth grade, when the elementary school faculty decreed that Mary Lee and Madrigal must have different teachers. The second week they gave up.

There was the time Mary Lee went shopping at the mall with Scarlett Maxsom, the way other girls did — with a friend. How strange it had been to have no twin along. To laugh with somebody whose laugh was not partly her own. She had had the fleeting thought that it would be fun to have a friend.

There was the sweet and funny afternoon that she and Van, Scarlett's brother, had had strawberry sundaes together. Not a date, really, just a lovely coincidence for Mary Lee to cherish.

In fact, the twins had never dated. They never did anything without each other. Their presence overwhelmed boys. Girls as beautiful and as incredibly alike as these two were not girls so much as an Event.

It was odd how that brief hour with Van had also acquired the status of an Event. She remembered it like a beloved movie, and replayed it in her heart, and even Madrigal did not know how often Mary Lee thought of that afternoon.

But the largest Event of her life was Separation. Already it had a capital letter: It was as huge as the sky and as impenetrable as marble.

"You are not to telephone," Mother and Father had said sternly. "You must write letters instead."

Not telephone? Not hear my sister's voice?

"I *have* to phone," pleaded Mary Lee. "I have to have something left." She turned to Madrigal. "Don't listen to them. Phone me anyway, when they're not home."

"I think they're right," said her twin.

The betrayal was so huge and painful that Mary Lee could not even think about it. She knew if Madrigal had fought back, Separation would not have occurred. But Madrigal had not fought back. Madrigal hadn't argued once. Not once. It was a slap that left a bruise on her heart. Once Mary Lee had the sick thought that her twin was not going to miss her. She killed that thought in a hurry!

Madrigal, left at home, would be as devastated as Mary Lee, shipped away.

She could not understand anything that was happening. Mother and Father actually seemed to hover over her that final week before she left home. As if she were in danger. As if people near her were unsafe. At night she wept into her pillow. In the morning, Mother's eyes were red, and Father's eyes were circled, but Madrigal's eyes were clear and bright.

How could it be? Mother and Father who had always seemed to love her so much had shuffled her off like an old deck of cards.

* * *

The mountains were high and crisp. Gray stone buildings sat on a wide grass campus. Thick dark woods enclosed the school like a fortress of old.

She was alone. It had never happened to her before. Ordinary people were often alone, but identical twins, never. What a hideous sensation it was — to be alone! How did people stand it? She was so glad not to be ordinary.

Identical twins, thank heaven, could communicate by invisible waves. Not ultraviolet, not X, not micro, not radio, but twin waves. Through the air and her soul, Mary Lee reached for her twin.

Nothing happened.

The waves were silent.

In her worst nightmares, Mary Lee had never expected this. Even if death were to come, she had expected to share it with Madrigal.

She was alone. And Madrigal had agreed to it.

Her father had actually had the nerve to cuddle her at the airport, to say good-bye privately, as if he were doing a good thing, a fatherly warm thing. "Be my brave soldier," he said to her.

Mary Lee hated that comparison.

"Put your best foot forward and try hard. Make friends. Stay alive."

My best feet walk in step with my twin's, she thought, fighting tears.

She crossed that school campus, and in the heavy grass left but one set of footprints. Neither of them looked like a best foot to Mary Lee. And what a queer trio of orders: try, make friends, stay alive. Of course she was going to stay alive. You didn't die of loneliness. Although no doubt she would feel dead, without Madrigal. As for "make friends," she didn't want any friend except Madrigal! As for "try" — well, yes, he was right about that. She did have to try. He was leaving her with no choice except trying.

It's too hard, she thought, already exhausted, and she hadn't even introduced herself to a single person.

The dormitory was large. So many strange girls to identify and names to learn. They seemed to know each other already, and have the passwords and jokes of intimate groups. The third floor, to which Mary Lee was assigned, seemed more a gathering of teams than a crowd of potential friends.

"Hi," she said to the girls, "I'm Mary Lee?" Her voice stumbled, the end of the sentence questioningly up in the air, for that was how it felt, not introducing Madrigal, too. Floaty and undecided. Half an introduction for half a set.

But all the girls had been new once, and they moved forward as if they expected to be best friends.

"I'm Bianca," said her first roommate, smiling.

"I'm Mindy," said her second roommate, and she actually swept Mary Lee into a hug.

"We're glad to have you," they both said. "We'll show you the ropes, because this is our third year here. They put you with us because we can help."

Okay, she said to herself. This won't be the end of the world. People are nice. Somehow I can survive.

The calendar of the school year stretched out hideously long. September until June? She couldn't go home until Christmas! Oh, that was evil, making her stay here four entire months by herself.

No matter how nice Mindy and Bianca were, Mary Lee could only half-respond. And it didn't help that, on the third floor, there was already a Marilyn, a Merrill, and a Mary. Mary Lee was yet another similar name to overload people's memories. Nobody could get her name right. Mindy and Bianca decided to call her ML.

It made her feel like a corporate logo, a piece of stock.

Madrigal I need you, she begged over the miles. But the twin waves remained silent.

It was worse than being alone: She felt unoccupied. A partly emptied mind and soul.

In the beginning, Mindy and Bianca escorted her everywhere, introducing her with smiles and hugs. But Mary Lee, homesick and heartsick, just stood there: the kind of boarder no school wants, because her only contribution is to lower morale.

The school year continued like a night without sleep.

Mary Lee had never had to make friends before. She had been equipped with an escort since birth. And even though she was so lonely her heart hurt, and she would have taken any pharmaceutical in production to ease the pain, she did not reach out.

Through the blinding loneliness, she saw that Mother and Father had been right: She was crippled by her twinness.

When Madrigal and Mary Lee sashayed into a room, action and speech ceased. People were fascinated. Twins are unusual. Identical twins are striking. Beautiful identical twins are an Event.

Mary Lee was just another pretty black-haired girl on a campus stocked with pretty girls. No longer an Event, she let herself become the reverse. A Non-Event.

At dinner, for which seats were assigned, companionship was enforced at a full table. But for breakfast and lunch, girls came when they were hungry, or awake. Some tables were empty while others were jammed. Mary Lee ached to join a packed table, yet sat at an empty one, yearning for the twin back home, for the life back home, the friends and school and parents and good things.

Whatever good there was at boarding school, Mary Lee ignored.

Within days she was branded: the sort of loser who sat alone; who had no friends and never would. Mindy and Bianca dutifully continued to be nice, and quietly asked the dorm mother if Mary Lee could be transferred to another room.

Mary Lee observed the dorm friendships. How lovely they were! How much Mary Lee wanted one for herself. If she had not had a twin, perhaps she would have possessed such a thing with Scarlett. Or Van. But the chance had gone by, she had been too absorbed by Madrigal to consider it, or to act upon it, and now Scarlett and Van and all that was home and good and safe were lost to her.

Among their other terrible orders when they enforced Separation, Mother and Father had ordered Mary Lee to tell nobody that she was an identical twin. "Am I supposed to hide it like some scandalous past?" she wept.

"No," said Father, "you're supposed to forget it, like some crippling past."

Forget that you were an identical twin? How could she?

In boarding school there was little history. It was as if they had all dumped something behind. They had all abandoned a twin or a parent or a past. They lived in the present, and Mary Lee's present did not include a twin. People didn't ask for background, and they quit asking Mary Lee anything.

When she thought of home — which was constantly — she thought mostly of questions she should have asked Mother and Father. There had to be more to this than they had explained. Why, if there had been too much togetherness, didn't they just make Mary Lee take different courses at school? Sign up for different sports? Get involved with different activities? Why couldn't she have gone to one of the private day schools in town — why pick a school nearly two thousand miles away?

Now and then Bianca and Mindy yelled at her, and told her to make an effort, and said if she was lonely it was her own fault.

My own fault, she thought. It must be all my fault, and none of Madrigal's fault, or Mother and Father wouldn't have done it this way. But what did I do?

She struggled to communicate with Madrigal by letter. The twins had certainly never written to each other before. In fact, they often skipped speaking. There was no need. They knew each other's thoughts and plans without speech.

One thousand nine hundred and twelve miles proved something terrible. Something Mary Lee would have been happier not knowing.

Dear Madrigal . . . wrote Mary Lee twice a week. What to say next? *It's terrible here; I miss you so; I want to come home!*

She couldn't write that. The whole point was that Mary Lee and Madrigal had passed the point of normalcy and must be separated to be whole. And what was this whining, but proof?

So Mary Lee wrote lies. *I am on the field hockey team*, she wrote, although she was not.

My roommates Mindy and Bianca are wonderful, she wrote. That much was true. It was Mary Lee who was not proving to be a wonderful roommate.

My English teacher, Mrs. Spinney, thinks

my writing is brilliant, she wrote, although Mrs. Spinney had given her C-minus on her last two papers.

Madrigal's letters were also full of lies.

She did not write nearly as often as Mary Lee. *I am having a great year. What a good idea this was! What wonderful times I'm having.*

No doubt Mother and Father supervised the writing of such paragraphs. She pictured them, ripping up the letter in which Madrigal wept and sobbed and confessed how awful it was without her twin, and dictating those hateful sentences: *I am having a great year. What a good idea this was! What wonderful times I'm having.*

Sometimes she remembered another sentence. Madrigal, Mother had said, will stay home under our supervision.

The twins had always behaved perfectly. When had they ever needed supervision?

Certainly boarding school was supervised. Mary Lee got used to it, as people get used to any form of torture. With cruel slowness, Christmas holidays inched closer.

Twenty days at home. Twenty days with Madrigal. Twenty days in which Mary Lee would not stand before a mirror, because she would be, and would have, a mirror. Her living twin. Her other self.

No one ever returned home from boarding school as joyfully as Mary Lee.

But it did not happen.

There stood the identical twin. Madrigal, her mirror, her lost fraction, remained lost. Mary Lee could no longer read Madrigal. She was no longer joined in heart and mind with this sister.

Mother and Father had accomplished their wish.

The twins were Separate.

When they were eleven, they had been forced to have separate bedrooms. It had taken them years to learn how to sleep with walls between them. Now the wall between them was invisible, but higher. The twins might as well have been divorced.

. . . *and Madrigal was glad.*

"But Madrigal," whispered Mary Lee. She was beyond heartsick. She was seasick, as if they stood on a tossing boat. "You must want me back!"

Her sister sighed. "Of course I do, MreeLee." MreeLee was Madrigal's baby nickname for Mary Lee. Madrigal kissed her, but it was a kiss of duty. A kiss because she had to.

"Why?" cried Mary Lee. "What's happened? I miss you so much! It's so hard, Madrigal. At school most of the day and night I try to hear you, but I don't get through! It's like being *anybody*."

Madrigal would comfort her now. Because that had been their special pride, their special secret. *We are not like anybody. We are us.*

"Life has changed," said her sister briefly.

Fear rose up like floodwater to drown Mary Lee. "But *we* haven't changed!"

Her sister's eyes moved in an expression Mary Lee could not duplicate. Mouth curved with an emotion Mary Lee did not know. Two words came out of her sister's mouth like spinning tops. "Jon Pear," said Madrigal. "My boyfriend. *Jon Pear.*"

Mary Lee was stunned.

Boyfriend? What boyfriend?

Had her identical twin mentioned Jon Pear in letters?

No.

Had Mother and Father mentioned that Madrigal had a boyfriend?

No.

Had Mary Lee felt that her sister had a man in her life?

No.

"I'd love to meet him," she said shyly. How

extraordinary, to be shy with her own twin!

Madrigal shook her head firmly. "He knows I have a twin," she said, "and I imagine people in school have told him we are identical. But I don't want him to see you. I want him to think only of me. Not a set of me."

"You don't want your boyfriend to meet me? I'm half of you!"

Madrigal made a face. "Don't be so melodramatic, MreeLee."

"But you're keeping me offstage! Hidden away, like a family scandal!" Mary Lee found herself fussing with her hair, poking at her buttons, tugging on her earrings. Not once did her twin move with her. The simultaneous broadcast had ceased.

"MreeLee," said her sister, being patient, putting up with her. "Come on now. Your girls' school has a companion boys' school. Boys are stacked ten deep just across the street from you. A thousand of them! Pick one."

"Of course I want a boyfriend," said Mary Lee, "but that has nothing to do with us. I want us."

Madrigal fixed her with a stare for which Mary Lee had no return. "I have a different *us* now, Mreelee," she said. "You are not to interfere."

Mary Lee could not think about this Jon

Pear, this different *us*. It was too huge and terrible. In only a few days she would be back at boarding school. She had to make Madrigal understand her desperation. "Madrigal, please visit me. Spend a long weekend with me. It would help if you came just for a little while."

"I'm busy," said Madrigal. "I have Jon Pear now, MreeLee. You've got to adapt. You even share the same ski slope with the boys' school. You ought to be able to meet someone cute. Trust me on this one. What you need is a boyfriend. Just pick one."

If she could pick, it would be Van. But she could not pick, for she did not go to the old high school, and would soon be shoved back on a plane and shipped away to boarding school. She could not pick there, either, where her uselessness hung around like negative ions.

Madrigal lost interest in Mary Lee's problems and left the house, and where she went, Mary Lee did not know, and could not feel; and when she came home, Madrigal did not tell.

"I hope you're happy," sobbed Mary Lee to her parents. "We're no longer identical. We're no longer a mixture. We're two instead of one."

"We aren't happy," said Father, "but we are right, Mary Lee."

A strange foggy sorrow seemed to envelope her parents. They hugged her, but distantly.

It went way beyond giving her away, they acted as if they had sold her into another world. Made a pact, a deal, and she would never know the terms. "What is happening?" she said brokenly. "Why are you doing this to me?"

"We are doing this *for* you, sweetheart," said her mother. "You must trust us."

Trust them? She actually laughed.

Christmas vacation ended.

Mary Lee was once again flying through gray skies with a gray heart.

Jon Pear, she thought. What is he like? And if he loves Madrigal, would he not love me exactly the same? For are we not exactly the same?

I wish, she said to the invisible stars behind the featureless clouds, *I wish for Madrigal's life.*

Chapter 2

"I'm coming," cried Madrigal on the telephone. "We'll go skiing! We'll have a lovely lovely time. I'll meet all your friends and gossip and we'll show off and be *us*."

"Mother and Father said you could come? Mother and Father said you could telephone?" whispered Mary Lee.

"No. They did not. But I love you, twin of mine, and you need me, and so I have arranged it in spite of them."

Oh, Madrigal! Mary Lee had given up hoping for a visit. Her heart had grown as cold as the February outdoors, and she had thought that only the arrival of summer vacation could end her loneliness.

She began laughing, planning, hoping. She pirouetted around her dorm. "Mindy, guess what! My identical twin is coming!"

Mindy had long since ceased to try with this

annoying personality-free roomie. "Give me a break. You don't have a twin."

"I do, I do! You'll love her." Mary Lee could not stop laughing. She felt thinner and lighter and giddier.

"You remembered this twin in *February*, ML?" Mindy exchanged skeptical looks with the ceiling. "Right."

"Right!" laughed Mary Lee.

The next day at meals, she assaulted tables and gatherings that she had ignored long enough that they now ignored her. "I'm an identical twin!" she cried. "And my twin is coming to visit for the three-day weekend!"

The popular girls exchanged long looks.

"It happens at this time of year," said Marilyn with a shrug. "Too much winter. The useless ones get crazy. They start believing in identical twins."

Mary Lee flushed.

The popular girls laughed, their mouths gaping. "So, Mary Lee," said one of Bianca's buddies, "if your supposed identical twin is *really* identical to you . . ." — A cruel smile flickered on the pretty round face — "like — who cares?"

"Stop," said Bianca, obeying the roommate rule. You stick up for your roommate even when she's a dork. "Leave Mary Lee alone."

(A skill, of course, that everyone was now pretty good at.)

Madrigal arrived.

She stalked onto that campus, and it was hers. She was the Event Mary Lee had longed to be. She overwhelmed the girls in Mary Lee's dorm and made them her own possessions. By the end of the very first evening, the twins were sitting at the very best table, among the most desirable girls. But it was Madrigal and Madrigal alone to whom they spoke.

Maddy, they said affectionately, come to our room and listen to tapes. Maddy, sit with us. Ski with us tomorrow, Maddy. Have hot chocolate with us, Maddy.

In spite of the identical look that had confused people for seventeen years at home, the girls on Third were able to tell Mary Lee and Madrigal apart. Mary Lee was shocked. Back home, she was always answering to Madrigal and Madrigal answering to Mary Lee. How could Bianca and Mindy and Merrill and Marilyn so easily know which dark skinned dark haired dark eyed beauty was Madrigal?

Madrigal had personality.

Mary Lee, whose school this was, remained wallpaper.

This visit for which Mary Lee had had such high hopes was the most horrible weekend of her life. She was taught a terrible and unwanted truth: It is *not* the surface that matters. For the surfaces of the twins were identical. In five months of living with them, she had displayed nothing to these girls. Twenty-four hours with Madrigal, and they had a best friend.

I am not identical. She is better. And everybody but me knew all along. It's why I was the one sent to boarding school — Mother and Father knew — Madrigal is the worthy one. I am nothing but an echo.

She tried to twin-wave this dreadful thought to Madrigal, so Madrigal would sweep her up in hugs and love, understand completely and deeply. She needed Madrigal to deny it and prove the silly theory wrong.

Madrigal, however, did not notice. The twin who should have instantly comprehended the situation was simply enjoying herself. Laughing away, having a good old time.

And at night, in the dorm, Madrigal on a lumpy guest cot — she refused offers of bunks — Madrigal entertained them with stories of high school. Of handsome wonderful Jon Pear, and their exciting wild dates. Of Jon Pear's romantic escapades and his crazy insane ideas.

It didn't even sound like home to Mary Lee. Mother and Father, who all but fingerprinted the kids their little girls played with, letting Madrigal go out at any hour of the day or night with this wild-acting Jon Pear? There seemed to be no curfews, no rules, no supervision.

Supervision. She remembered that word. Mother had claimed to keep Madrigal at home for "supervision."

"Wow, you get to do *anything*, don't you?" said Bianca enviously. She brushed Madrigal's gorgeous fall of black hair, playing with it and fixing it, as if this were an incredible treat, as if Mary Lee, with the same hair, had not been around all year.

Sunday was the final day of a too long and too lonely visit. Mary Lee said to her sister, "I'm not going to ski today. You go on with Bianca and Mindy. I'm going to work on my report."

They were fixing each other's hair as they often had, a perfect reflection of the other without mirrors. Mary Lee stared at her lovely self; and at the self who was actually somebody else. Those hazel green eyes, so clear and true — so deep and unreadable. That rich olive skin, like a curtain between them. The long black lashes, finer than any mascara, dropping like a fringe to separate their lives. Each girl had caught her heavy black hair back twice, high on top of the head, and again low at the neck.

Who are you? thought Mary Lee. *I don't even know you!*

"Of course you're going to ski," said Madrigal. "That's what's across the street. A ski slope. So you ski. Don't be such a baby, MreeLee."

"I'm not as coordinated as you are," said Mary Lee.

Her sister poked her. "We are identical in leg muscles, too," said Madrigal. "Now we're going to ski. There are people out there I intend to impress. Two of us are more impressive than one of us."

Who is out there for you to impress? thought Mary Lee. You own them all already.

It would happen, though. They would go out there, the two of them, and only one of them — Madrigal — would impress somebody.

Madrigal's ski outfit was stunning.

Jacket and pants looked as if they had begun life as a taffeta Christmas ball gown: darkly striking crimson and green plaid with black velvet trim and black boots. Madrigal was no oddity, but a trendsetter. Every other girl on the slopes was now out of date.

Including Madrigal's twin.

For Mary Lee wore the same neon solids everyone else had that winter: Hers was turquoise. The color, which had seemed so splendid, which would hold its own against the lemon-yellow and hot-orange and lime-green of other skiiers, was now pathetically out of style.

She was ashamed of her turquoise. She felt obvious. She felt loud and lacking in taste.

In fact, Mary Lee felt like an imposter. As if she and her sister had not started life as equally divided halves; as if Madrigal had drawn nine tenths of the personality, and Mary Lee the slight remaining fraction.

They could both wear their hair in the same black cloud of excitement, paint their lips the same dark rose, throw back their heads to laugh the same laugh . . . but even identical, Madrigal was more.

Despair overtook Mary Lee. She prayed that Madrigal was not reading her mind right now. What if Madrigal knew Mary Lee was eaten with jealousy over her own twin?

She thought to herself: Okay, this is my fault, this loneliness at school. It was a decision I stupidly made, not to try my hardest, not to be my best. But how can I start over? How do I make friends where I shrugged them off before?

Madrigal did not waver in her affection. Even now, during the mild argument that was the closest they had ever come to fighting,

Madrigal tilted forward to touch her twin's cheek with her lips.

"Okay, okay," said Mary Lee reluctantly, breaking down, "we'll ski. But you'd better break your leg in the same place I break mine, Madrigal."

Madrigal laughed. "I have too much at stake to allow for hospital time."

She meant Jon Pear.

Mary Lee's cheeks grew hot. Unwanted jealousy whipped like an approaching blizzard through the snow of her heart.

Perhaps that was the great difference that people saw or suspected. Perhaps having a boy in your life lifted your spirits so high that everyone else wanted to hang onto the edge of your soaring heart. Take a free ride to love.

Mary Lee no longer knew what love was. Her twin had discarded her, her parents had shipped her away. If you could not trust the love of your family, could you trust the love of some unknown boy, or of anyone?

The mountain on which they skied rose beyond the playing fields. Girls supposedly came to the school for the famous academics, but as far as Mary Lee could tell, they came for the nearby boys and the winter sports. The two schools shared an indoor skating rink, so figure skating and ice hockey could be practiced year round. Each ski team could be at the top of the mountain within minutes of the end of classes.

So while there were several hundred girls that Mary Lee had failed to impress, there were also several hundred boys. Could Madrigal have her eyes on one of them? Why would somebody as deeply in love with a boy as Madrigal said she was with Jon Pear look at anyone else?

What was Jon Pear like? What if she met a boy as wonderful as Jon Pear? For he must be wonderful, or Madrigal would not adore him so.

"Do you and Jon Pear talk about me?" she said, wanting to be a necessary part of her sister's conversation with Jon Pear.

Madrigal turned away from the twin who looked exactly like her to look in the mirror instead. When she spoke, her generous lips played with the single word and lingered upon it. "No."

Madrigal smiled into the mirror and the mirror, of course, smiled back, equally satisfied. Madrigal's lips moved, and Mary Lee read them: *Mirror, Mirror, On the Wall, Who Is the Fairest of Them All?*

Mary Lee was chilled. The mirror cannot answer that question, she thought. We are equally fair.

Another word from Mother's lecture flickered in Mary Lee's memory like a reminder on the calendar: *unhealthy*.

"But Jon Pear must wonder what it's like," said Mary Lee quickly. "Everybody wants to know what it's like to be identical twins."

"I'm sure he does," said Madrigal, giving her twin a hard look, "but he has the good manners not to refer to it."

Mary Lee was cut to the bone.

"I don't think he actually believes that I could have an identical twin," said Madrigal, laughing now. She seemed to flirt with her reflection. "He's in love with me. He says, *'Two of Madrigal? Impossible.'*" Madrigal went on ahead, dancing out the dormitory door in her dashing glittering ski suit. She was greeted with cries of ecstasy and friendship from girls who had never bothered with Mary Lee.

"Oh, Madrigal! This is such fun!"

"How neat to be an identical twin!"

"Tell us all about it. What's it really like?"

They did not ask Mary Lee what it was like.

Mary Lee became part of the masses, blending in with ordinary skiiers, while Madrigal was fascinating and special and An Identical Twin.

The boarding school's bus carried the skiiers and their equipment the single mile to the lifts.

Everybody got out, carefully manuevering long skis and poles and making put-your-eye-out jokes.

Madrigal scampered ahead of Mary Lee. Way ahead. Deep in a throng of new, but close, friends. Laughing and teasing and thoroughly enjoying herself.

Mary Lee pulled out an old ugly knit cap and stuffed her heavy hair beneath it. The cap was not a good match for the turquoise ski suit; it was royal blue: together the colors snarled. Mary Lee became plain. An inconvenient blue splat.

She struggled even to trudge in her sister's wake, her abandoned heart no longer pumping as it should.

Halfway to the lifts, Madrigal paused. Around her, the crowd had expanded as if it were being multiplied by some geometric factor; as if some magic algebra class were using the creatures on this slope for their problematic equations, moving and multiplying what had once been human beings.

Fear clogged Mary Lee's arteries and thoughts.

Mary Lee, came a pulsing wordless communication. *Come.*

Madrigal was calling. The lovely unspoken words had returned.

Madrigal just figured out how lonely and lost I am without her. So we're back. Twins again, touching without speech again!

Madrigal entered the immense lodge, and Mary Lee flew in the building, too, broken heart mending as she ran.

"*I knew you'd come.*" They said it together, inflections on the same syllables, lips equally lingering on the *m*.

Madrigal huffed out a breath of relief. "I was afraid we'd lost it, MreeLee."

"Me, too," said Mary Lee, her eyes filling.

The twins embraced. The joy was almost too much to bear.

Madrigal pushed Mary Lee into a girls' room. "I feel so bad because you have on that old rag of a ski suit and I've got such a beauty. Listen, MreeLee."

Mary Lee's heart turned over with love for this twin who outshone her.

"We'll switch," said Madrigal. "You be the star here. This is your school. I don't know what's the matter with me, trying to leap into your life as well as my own."

How she loved this sister, who would come through for her in the end. We're still twins, Mary Lee thought, passionately relieved. "It's okay," she said. "You look perfect in it."

Madrigal giggled. "Then so would you, Miss Identical Twin."

They undressed with lightning speed, the way they had since they were toddlers. "You be Madrigal, MreeLee," said her twin, zipping Mary Lee into the gleaming taffeta plaid.

"What do you mean?"

"We'll switch." Madrigal's wild smile demanded a return, and Mary Lee gave it, smiling wildly back, though comprehending nothing.

"You join them as Madrigal. You answer when they say Maddy. You be the one they want. You laugh and ski and be silly with them. You have hot chocolate and listen to tapes and dance in the dark as their brand-new extra-special-Event friend." Madrigal yanked the ugly blue cap down over *her* hair this time. "Then tonight, when they've completely confused which of us is which, we'll tell who's who. It'll be hysterical. Everybody will have a good laugh. It'll help. I promise. It'll get you started up again, like a stalled motor."

Madrigal lifted her hands to hold her sister's, and, of course, her sister's hands had lifted at the same second to hold hers. In the unfathomable way of identical minds, they had each chosen to wear a silver ring on the third finger of the right hand, to wear clear polish, no watch, and two slim silver bracelets.

Madrigal pushed Mary Lee gently in the small of her back, sending her sister out into the group, shining like a Christmas decoration.

Mary Lee was enveloped in Third Floor girls. Mindy and Bianca and Marilyn cried, "Madrigal! What happened to you? Where'd you go?"

"Come on!"

"Time's wasting!"

"Snow's melting!"

So many exclamation points. So much excitement. All because they thought she was somebody else.

Chapter 3

With so many friends clustered around her, the new Madrigal was slow to reach the ski lift. Girls bumped companionably against her, and giggled, and offered sticks of gum or candy. Where once they had seemed sharks swarming, chewing at her with cruel appetites, they were now pleasant smiling girls having a good time together.

Is there a lovelier word in the English language, thought Mary Lee, than *friends*?

A shock of disloyalty hit her. Of course there was a lovelier word than *friends*. *Twins* was lovelier; lovelier by far.

She looked to see where the new Mary Lee was, but her twin, since she was alone, and therefore able to wriggle through the crowds, had actually arrived first at the chair lift. In spite of such a crush of people waiting in line, no one stepped up to share the seat with the new Mary Lee.

Alone, swinging on the chair lift, went the turquoise suit and the ugly blue cap. The lift careened forward several feet, jerked to a partial stop, and then jerked on. The head of the girl jerked with it, as if on a stem, not a neck.

Not one other person at the mountain was all by herself.

She felt terribly, desperately, sorry for that girl.

You're Madrigal right now, Mary Lee reminded herself. Stop worrying about that loser. Tonight she'll evaporate. You'll dispose of pitiful Mary Lee. You'll be popular, identical-twinned Mary Lee.

Mindy pushed the group to the head of the lift line, talking and laughing. Mindy, the roommate who still wanted to eat with her, still trudged to the library with her, still cheerfully yelled her name across the campus. "Madrigal, we have another long weekend in March," said Mindy. "Won't you visit then? Or — I know! Would you like to visit me over spring vacation? We'll be going to the islands, of course. You don't need a tan, you were born with the perfect tan, but I'm hideous and have to spruce up my skin. You'll come, won't you."

Mindy spoke with the complete assurance of

one who knows her invitation is irresistable.

"Honestly, Madrigal," said Bianca, "you really floored us when we found out there was an identical twin."

"You're not like your sister at all," said Mindy.

"You," pointed out Bianca, "are interesting."

Mary Lee killed time by yanking the ribbons out of her hair and letting her black tresses spread in the wind. Far ahead and up the mountain, her twin reversed the hair motion, tucking hers even more completely up under the blue cap. Pretty gleaming ski costumes by the dozen shone around, and the girl they thought was Mary Lee stood out like a mistake.

"It's amazing that you and your twin could be so different," said Mindy.

They don't bother to use the name Mary Lee, thought Mary Lee. I'm not even a name to them. I'm a person not worth naming.

She willed them to say "Mary Lee" out loud, but they did not.

"I wish you were the one at school here, Madrigal," said Bianca. "We'd have so much fun."

The snow seemed to laugh. The entire mountain shook its head and snickered. The terrible cliff below the ski lifts was not rimmed with crags and rocks, but the razor teeth of sharks.

It's too late, thought Mary Lee. I can't get another chance. I've ruined it for Mary Lee. She isn't interesting and she isn't worth inviting anywhere.

Once these girls knew the truth, they would moan and groan and scatter. There would be no lasting friendships. Oh, Madrigal would get away with it; they would think she was funny; clever, even, to have pulled off such good mimicry. But the moment Madrigal left, Mary Lee's life would be empty once more.

I don't want Mindy and Bianca to like me because I'm somebody else. I really do want to be a separate person, the way Mother and Father said we need to be; and I want to be a *likeable* separate person. With friends of my own.

She truly saw the light, as if the snow and the sun had been laid out today to clear her eyes.

Mother and Father had been right; acting in kindness, not cruelty. Twinship had gotten unhealthy — two living and breathing and moving as one.

Next three-day weekend, she decided, I'll go home. Argue with Mother and Father. Reverse their decision. Agree to anything. I'll play horrible sports like field hockey and take hideous subjects like History of the Cold War. I'll take over cleaning the toilets and learn how to change the oil in the cars. Anything. I just want to go home.

The sun hit the snow so hard, even sunglasses were no help. The glittering rays were as hard as metal.

The lifts continued to deposit skiers at the top of the mountain, and groups continued to spill out, ski down, whirl and flourish on the snow. A group in scarlet and black; a family whose children did not bother with poles; a row of brawny men, whose weight would surely crush the skis instead of cross the snow.

And then a pause.

A pause in which Mary Lee's yearning to go home was so immense, so filling, it seemed to her it was written on the sky, as well as in her heart.

A pause in which the Mary Lee who was actually Madrigal seemed for a moment stuck on the lift. Stuck alone and friendless. Perhaps equally stuck in life.

The gondola in which the twin sat by herself leaped forward again, and the thin metal rod that curved over the top of the seat and held the gondola to the cables, snapped. Over the roar of the snowmakers and the shouts of the skiers, no sound was audible.

The gondola flipped, as if unearthly hands were shaking the contents out. The contents that were Mary Lee's twin. Skis tangled, turquoise legs twisted, a knit cap caught on the protective bar, but the girl herself fell like a silent stone.

Madrigal! My twin! No!

"No!" screamed Mary Lee. She could not run. She wore skis. She who spoke to her twin without words shrieked every word she knew to stop the falling. "No! Hang on! Don't fall!" She kicked one foot free of the thick shining ski boot, planning to burst away from Bianca and Mindy, run faster than anyone could, get beneath her tumbling sister, catch her, save her —

But she did not even get the second boot off.

Her twin's body spiralled only once, and then, headfirst, fell prisoner to gravity. Not on soft snow, not neatly feet first, not easily into cushioning hands, but viciously, cruelly, horribly onto the rock scree which divided the bunny slope from the advanced.

The end of identical twins took only a moment.

The mountain had had no respect for their twinship. The rocks had not cared. Gravity had not given it a second thought.

* * *

Slick steep snow. So easy to ski down. So hard to run up. The gondola itself did not fall all the way, but hung, like a loose tooth, swinging lightly in the wind. Occupied by a ghost skiier.

"Don't look!" cried Mindy, holding her back.

"You mustn't go over there," said Bianca forcefully, pushing her away.

Mary Lee fought them. "It's my sister," she panted, "it's my twin."

The ski instructors turned swiftly into an emergency crew.

She has to be alive, thought Mary Lee. If Madrigal died, I would die, too. I feel it. My heart would stop, my brain would darken. So she's alive, because I am.

The place filled with grown-ups of the most obnoxious kind. People trying to make her go into the lodge and sit down. People trying to block her view. People saying she couldn't help. "Stop this!" she shrieked at them, pummeling with her fists, kicking with her fat, useless boots. "Let me through!"

They were too padded to feel her blows, and the boots were too heavy for her to bruise any shins. She might have been a rag doll for all she accomplished.

Mrs. Spinney, who coached the girls' ski team as well as teaching English, skiied right down into the group. "Who was hurt?" she shouted, clutching at everybody.

"Mary Lee," said Bianca. "Oh, Mrs. Spinney, it was Mary Lee, and she was never happy here." Bianca began crying horribly.

The rescue crew had an orange sled, long and scooped out, like an Indian canoe, and into this they strapped the victim. When the rescuers dragged the sled the rest of the way down the slope, people drew back, as if in the presence of something special. And they were. For whoever had lived and breathed, whoever had suffered and rejoiced, no longer occupied that body. The girl on the stretcher was only a series of rises beneath a dark brown blanket.

"Is she — ?" began Mrs. Spinney. "Is she — ?"

"Dead," whispered Bianca.

Dead.

Mary Lee tried to think about that word, but it could not have a connection to her and her family. Certainly not to her twin. The high scream of the siren seemed very important. They were rushing to save Madrigal, of course. Because they had to save Madrigal, of course. Because this was her identical twin, of course, and life could not go on for Mary Lee unless Madrigal were there.

The headmaster of the boys' school was the

most senior available adult. "Madrigal?" he said to her gently.

She shook her head. "Mary Lee."

"Yes," he said. "Mary Lee had a terrible accident. Mary Lee" — even the headmaster, who had been in Vietnam, and whose gory stories thrilled his boys, had trouble ending the sentence. But he did — "is dead."

"No," she said numbly. "No, she's not. You see . . ."

But he did not see. He decided it would be best for her grieving process (he actually said this) for her to look upon and touch the body of her sister, to see the terrible wounds and know that her sister really was dead.

This turned out not to be the right step in the grieving process, for the remaining twin began shrieking and sobbing when she saw the ruin that had been her darling sister. "No, no, no!" screamed Mary Lee.

When the ambulance arrived, the crew assessed the situation and took the living sister, not the dead one, to the hospital.

"Now, Maddy," said the nurse soothingly. "Your friends are all here, waiting to sit with you. We've phoned your parents, and they're arranging a flight to get here. This little shot will just relax you enough to get you through the rest of the night, that's all."

"Mary Lee," she said for the thousandth time.

"Yes," agreed the nurse. "It's very very sad. I'm not a twin, myself, although I always wanted to be, you know, and when I was pregnant each time, I said to myself, I said, maybe it'll be twins. I would have loved twins."

The shot took effect very fast, and Mary Lee, swirling down into the darkness, thought perhaps death had felt like this. A swirling down. Perhaps at the bottom she would find Madrigal, or perhaps she was asleep during this, dreaming a terrible cruel nightmare, and the swirling would waken her, and Madrigal would be there, laughing and lovely.

I'll have to tell Jon Pear, thought Mary Lee, just before she lost awareness. He loves her, and I'll have to tell him she no longer exists.

The tranquilizer was worthy of the name. She slipped into the comfort of knowing nothing.

When Mary Lee awoke in the morning, she was in a vanilla-plain room, under crispy sheets, with white waffled blankets. Next to her bed was its identical twin. White and waffled. Waiting.

I want Madrigal in that bed, thought Mary Lee. I want Madrigal to be alive. I want the ski slope to be a nightmare. Is this the psych ward? If I've done something terrible or shameful, it's okay, as long as my twin is alive.

A nurse walked in, smiling. A doll-like smile, pursed and red. "Good morning, Maddy."

"Mary Lee," she said for the hundredth time.

The nurse was followed by a doctor, and the two women looked weirdly alike, the same steady lipsticky smile coating the doctor's face.

"Yes," said the doctor, taking Mary Lee's hand as if to console her, but turning her wrist and taking her pulse instead. "Mary Lee is dead, Maddy. It's a terrible tragedy. Mom and Dad are on their way. I spoke to them last night."

How blurry and strange this was. The twins had never called Mother "Mom" and never called Father "Dad." The family never called Madrigal Maddy, either.

"Did you tell my parents that Mary Lee died?" said Mary Lee, even more heartsick. This was terrible. She could at least have called Mother and Father herself. What a weakling she was. Poor Mother and Father were sitting on some plane even now, picturing the wrong daughter dead on a slab.

Madrigal, or what was left of her, probably

lay somewhere in this very hospital. They would have taken off the ugly turquoise ski suit and put her into — no. She would be wearing nothing. It would not matter at all that her bare flesh was against cold steel. Madrigal would never know anything again.

This was so horrible, Mary Lee could not stand being in the building. "I need to go back to the school," she said, weeping without brushing her cheeks.

"Good for you," said the doctor. "That's what we want, Maddy. Courage to face this. Identical twins! My, my. It's a double whammy for you. Now, your sister's roommates are coming to pick you up. Bianca and Mindy will be here in a minute and they'll stay with you all day. You don't need to worry about being alone, Maddy, until Mom and Dad get here."

"I'm Mary Lee," she said tiredly. "You see — "

The doctor hushed her. "Mom and Dad already talked to me about the problem," she said. "You two were over-identifying. It happens. Parents make mistakes, and Mom and Dad made their share. Identical twins aren't easy to bring up, and separating you two was very wise. It's just a terrible shame the equipment snapped. Let's not blame Mom and Dad."

Mary Lee thought that, next time it

snapped, maybe the equipment should be holding this doctor.

Bianca and Mindy crept into the room like great big fashionable mice. "Maddy?" they whispered.

It was too much to fight off. Why argue with Mindy and Bianca? Why argue with anybody? In a few hours Mother and Father would arrive, and they would know the instant they were in the room with her that she was —

— *the daughter they had not wanted to keep at home.*

The daughter who had died was the one they had cherished more.

Could she bear to see the shock in Mother's eyes — that it was Madrigal who had died? Could she bear to see the jolt in Father's face — that they were left with Mary Lee?

A dread even more cold and horrid than her twin's death enveloped her. What if Mother and Father wished that she, Mary Lee, *had* been the one on the gondola? What if, when they realized Mary Lee was alive and well . . . what if they were sorry?

She walked numbly between Bianca and Mindy. They had not thought to bring her a change of clothing, and she had to wear the ski suit that was Madrigal's. When they finally reached the dorm — interrupted by a hundred

47

people crying, "We're so sorry; Oh, this is awful; Oh, what a tragedy; Oh, poor Maddy, you lost your sister, we're so sorry about Mary Lee, Maddy" — she wanted only to shut the door and be alone.

But boarding schools are not arranged for alone-ness.

She stripped off Madrigal's ski suit and thought that when she got home she would burn it, for it did not deserve to live, when Madrigal could not. She opened her closet to find something plain and dark to wear. Perhaps her black T-shirt with the pleated pocket and her black jeans.

"Maddy!" said Bianca. "That's sick. You can't start by dressing in your sister's clothes." Bianca flipped open the suitcase that Madrigal had brought. "Here. Wear this cute little skirt."

"I'll wear the jeans," said Mary Lee wearily. "Bianca, I appreciate your concern, but I'd rather be alone."

"We can't let you be alone," said Mindy. "We promised the doctor."

"Promised her why?"

"Because she doesn't want you to think of following your sister. She says identical twins can get a little screwy."

Following my sister, thought Mary Lee. *If*

only you could do that! I would follow her and bring her back. I would —

They meant suicide. They had been told to stay with her to prevent her from killing herself.

"I'm not the type," said Mary Lee, "and neither was my sister. She loved life."

"Actually, she wasn't very happy," said Bianca.

"And she sure didn't love life here," added Mindy.

MreeLee, you be Madrigal.

And she was. Clothing was all it took.

Mindy and Bianca talked on and on, sure that it was Madrigal to whom they offered comfort.

Mary Lee wanted her parents desperately. She stood by the window, waiting and watching. They would come in an airport taxi. It would be orange. She would see it against the snow. She would run to her mother and be hugged; turn to her father and be held.

Nothing could bring Madrigal back home.

But surely, surely, there would be enough love left to bring Mary Lee back home!

Chapter 4

From the dorm window, she watched the orange taxi pull up in front of the administration building. Her mother and father got out. The Dean of Students walked swiftly down his wide stone steps, hand extended to shake theirs, as if congratulating them on the death of a twin. Everybody nodded heads up and down and then shook heads back and forth: a strange head-dance upon the mysteries of death.

Her parents were frail black outlines against the harsh glitter of snowbanks. Clinging to each other, they followed the Dean into his office. From the Dean, they would learn the details of the accident, be told exactly how their daughter died, exactly what arrangements had been made.

"Now, Madrigal," said Bianca, "be brave for your parents. They're going to need you."

"At least they have you," said Mindy. "It's

a terrible thing to lose a daughter, but then again, Mary Lee must have been the daughter they didn't much — "

"*Mindy!*" said Bianca. "Sssssshhh."

"I just meant that when you send one twin to boarding school and keep the other one at home with you, it could mean that — "

"Mindy!" said Bianca. "Shut up."

But it's true, thought Mary Lee. It was Mary Lee they disposed of. Now they just have to dispose of her again.

She began shivering, waves of cold passing through her and over her, as if she were sea water, going through a tide. Bianca yanked a blanket off her bed and wrapped her in it. "Poor Maddy," whispered Bianca. "Be brave."

I could have been friends with this nice girl, thought Mary Lee, and I didn't try. I wanted to be an Event without trying.

Mree Lee, you be Madrigal.

What did that mean?

She knew, because her sister had been sane, that Madrigal had not meant to die; had not meant that her twin should actually step into her life. But the opportunity was here. Perhaps the need was here. What if her parents really did need Madrigal . . . and did not need, and did not want, Mary Lee?

For one terrible sick moment, Mary Lee actually considered going on with the pretense that she was Madrigal.

For one terrible sick moment, Mary Lee saw herself in Madrigal's life: at home, popular, dating Jon Pear, the only daughter, the light of her parents' world.

How much better *that* life would be than the one she had now! How much more fun and exciting! How much more —

Mary Lee buried her face in the blanket. She had learned a great deal during this hard year. She knew more about who she was, and who she wanted to be. Throw that away? Be somebody else?

But of course, it was only halfway somebody else. Mary Lee was, even with death between them, an overlapping fraction with her identical twin.

She dropped the blanket and looked into the large three-way mirror that stood on top of Mindy's desk. Mindy never studied at her desk. She studied lying on her bed. The desk was for makeup.

The girl who looked back at Mary Lee, eyes swollen from weeping, looked — of course — exactly like Madrigal. Nobody would ever know if . . .

Nonsense. Mother gave birth to me. She will

know! I'm her baby, her daughter, her first-born, in fact, because I came twenty-four minutes before Madrigal.

Across the campus, the door to the administration building opened, and Mother, Father, and the Dean emerged. Slowly, tiredly, whipped by grief and shock, her parents made their way after the Dean toward the dormitory and their remaining daughter.

But what do I do, if she doesn't know? What if my own mother comes to hug me and cannot tell which twin I am? What if I have to introduce myself? Hi, Mother, I'm Mary Lee.

Mree Lee, you be Madrigal.

She tried to think of the essential morality of it. Was it amoral to shift into another person's life and clothes, name and world? Was it what Madrigal would have wanted? Was it what Mother and Father would want?

She tried to imagine taking on Madrigal's life.

Another loophole came to mind. The boyfriend!

Of course, Jon Pear would know. Whereas she wouldn't even recognize Jon Pear! In a heartbeat, he'd be able to tell that she had no memories of their dates; that those lips might look the same as the ones he had kissed, but these lips had never kissed a boy ever, let alone him.

She tried to visualize Jon Pear, but could think only of Scarlett's brother, Van. Immediately, she missed Van. He was the boy next door; he was the birthday cake and the soft icing; he was the summer wind and the new leaf.

Scarlett and Van were not twins, and yet both were seniors. Van had been kept back in first grade because he was hyperactive and the second-grade teachers didn't want him yet. Nobody would know it now. He had become the preppy type, with friends named Geordie and Kip. He played water polo and wore blue blazers with khaki pants, and his thin blond hair was smooth silk across his high forehead.

How can I be daydreaming about Van, she thought, when my sister is dead?

She wondered if Jon Pear knew. If the news had broken publicly. Was he even now screaming in the agony of loss, asking himself, "Why couldn't it have been the other one — that twin — that sister we never bothered to talk about?"

But, of course, Jon Pear thought it *was* the sister. Everybody thought it was the sister.

Her parents had reached the dorm, and the

Dean had gotten to the door first and was holding it for them.

Mary Lee faced the door like a captured prisoner facing the judge. She would leave it to fate. To chance. To Mother and Father.

If they opened the door and knew — knew that she was Mary Lee — knew who had lived and who had died — well, then, she would be Mary Lee.

But if they did not . . .

If Mary Lee was so inconsequential to them that they did not feel, did not see, did not instantly know . . .

Mree Lee, you be Madrigal.

. . . then she would be Madrigal.

Bianca rushed out to meet them. Perhaps she thought a good roomie had a duty to introduce herself to the bereaved parents. "Maddy is so upset," cried Bianca. "Thank goodness you're here. She needs you so."

Who could this person be, that Bianca called Maddy? Mother and Father wouldn't even know the nickname!

Madrigal, don't be mad at me! Whatever happens now, please forgive me. Forgive me for being the one who gets life.

The door opened.

Mother came in first. There was a strange light in her eyes. With a desperate sort of hope, she faced her living child. What do you hope for, Mother? thought Mary Lee. I want to give you what you want! I love you so. You choose here. I will be the daughter you want to have alive.

But Mother did not speak. She held out her arms, instead; her wonderful arms, the arms of comfort and love and assurance. Mary Lee rushed forward, sinking into her mother's embrace. Inside those arms, the world was safe and good; nobody died, and nobody got hurt. "Oh, Mother," she whispered. "Oh, Mother."

Father put his ten fingers into her hair, as he always had, gripping her fiercely like a caveman parent.

"You saw it happen, sweetie?" he said. "Was it terrible? Was it quick? Did she cry out?"

She could not speak. Her throat filled with the horror and she could only weep. Who am I? she thought. Tell me who I am.

Locked between her parents, she waited to hear a name. It was like waiting to be christened; waiting to be graduated.

"We've been staying with Madrigal," said Mindy.

"We didn't want Madrigal to be alone," added Bianca.

"We'd be glad to pack up her belongings for you to take back," said Mindy. "I'm a very good packer. It comes from living abroad so much. And Madrigal shouldn't have to do it."

"Or if there's too much pain involved," said Bianca, "we could arrange to take them to the Salvation Army."

Mother said, "We're thankful for all you did for both our girls. If you'd pack Mary Lee's things, that would help. Just ship everything home."

Mary Lee stepped away from Mother and Father. They were in agreement with Mindy and Bianca. It was Mary Lee who had died, and whose things must be packed, must be shipped as easily as once they had shipped the girl herself.

Her mother gave a funny little sigh and her father a strange little shiver. They did not hug her again. When she was able to see past the blur of fear, her parents were looking into the open closet of the daughter they thought dead: the clothes of Mary Lee. The stacked books, the open assignments, the tumbled sweaters, the precious jewelry.

The Dean said, "Madrigal?"

She felt herself within her skin, behind her eyes, under her hair. She felt her soul and her past. Shall I be Mary Lee? she asked herself in the silence of her fright.

The Dean repeated, "Madrigal?"

With eyes so afraid they went blind, she faced a future and a past. I am dead, thought Mary Lee. Madrigal lives. She said to the walls and the witnesses, "Yes."

Chapter 5

On the long and largely silent flight home, she stayed inside her mind and thought of Madrigal. There would be a funeral . . . but Madrigal's name would not be mentioned. Were you well and truly on your way to the next world if they buried you under another name? Would Madrigal forgive Mary Lee for this? Would Madrigal want this strange immortality; this life of hers that went on without her?

The steward gave her a tiny, white foam pillow, about the right size for a newborn baby, and into this pillow Mary Lee spilled her tears and behind this pillow Mary Lee hid her eyes.

Madrigal, how can I go on without you?

Is this how?

By becoming you?

She could not seem to talk to her parents. She recognized them; they were indeed Mother and Father. And yet strangers. How could parents not know their child?

She wanted fiercely to hear her mother call her Mary Lee . . . but what if her mother didn't mind that Mary Lee was gone. . . . What if Mother could not bear it that she had lost Madrigal?

Over and over, terrible conflicting thoughts tumbled through her mind, and over and over were swept away by torrents of tears for the twin she no longer had.

When the long day was over, and they had reached home, she remembered to enter not her own half-empty room, but Madrigal's full and busy one. She brushed her hair not with her own brush, but with the one lying carelessly on Madrigal's chest of drawers.

"Good night, Madrigal," said her father.

"Good night, Father."

"Will you be all right, Madrigal?" asked her mother.

"Yes, Mother. Will you be all right?"

They stared at each other, the remaining pieces of their family of four, the way you would stare at a person who had lost a limb. Where is his arm? you would think, wrenching your eyes away. Where is his leg?

Where is my twin? thought Mary Lee.

* * *

The sharing of mind and skin continued to the final instant of her sister's physical existence on earth. Her parents chose cremation. "I don't want you to do that!" Mary Lee had cried hysterically.

"Some things," said Father, "must be . . ." He paused, and his pause was heavy, and in the thick creamy silence she knew as if Father had been her twin what word he meant to use — *destroyed* — but he substituted; he said " . . . finished."

Cremation.

One-and-a-half hours of burning in a furnace. The waves of heat and terror were unspeakable.

She felt them both.

Mother and Father said it was not possible, but they knew nothing; they never had; they were ordinary people; they were not *us*.

I am not dead, Mary Lee thought, and yet she felt dead; she felt burned and ashy and scattered in the wind.

The names Madrigal and Mary Lee collided with each other, and hurt, like cutting knives. She did not know what to call herself in her heart.

Her heart hurt, her wrists and ankles and knees hurt, her head hurt, her throat hurt.

She was so very alone.

If she had thought herself separated from Madrigal by one thousand nine hundred and twelve miles, it was nothing compared to the separation of death.

She could not cry enough to rid herself of all the tears, and still the aching came on, traveling from one joint to another.

The memorial service was packed. So many students were there. She was a teenager herself, and knew teenagers. Many had come because it was a school day, and they wanted to get out of class. Many had come because death fascinated them. They wanted to see how it was done. Many had come because identical twins fascinated them, and they wanted to see what was left. Many had come because they wanted to see Madrigal in her new life, and wanted to console her. And perhaps a few . . . but what few? For her only friend had been her twin . . . had come to say good-bye to Mary Lee.

She sobbed for the girl who was not having a funeral . . . for no one knew she was dead. Could Madrigal rest? No words had been said over Madrigal; they were expended on Mary Lee, who lived.

She sat listening to her heart beat, wearing Madrigal's pretty black swirly skirt and Madrigal's gauzy white blouse and Madrigal's shining black heels. At the last moment she had added Madrigal's sunglasses, pretending she had to hide her red-rimmed weeping eyes. She was hiding Mary Lee's red-rimmed weeping eyes.

From behind the dark glasses, when they stood in the receiving line, she stared at every person her age. But the teenagers did not go through the line. Perhaps they lacked experience at funerals, or had bad manners, or were afraid to talk of death. For not one fellow student came up to shake hands, to hug, or to speak.

If she had not had the glasses to hide behind, she would have sobbed all over again. Mary Lee is dead! she thought. Can't you tell me you're sorry? You think it's me! Don't I matter even one sentence worth? Can't you put yourself out long enough to say you're sorry about Mary Lee?

But people hardly mentioned Mary Lee. Even dead, she was the other twin. The sent-away twin. Her parents' friends and the parents of the kids her age patted her shoulder. "Poor Madrigal," they said, "you must be brave." And then they said to Mother and Father, "This is so awful. We're so sorry. What can we do to help?"

But nobody could think of anything anybody

could do to help. Death has that quality of being beyond help. And so her mother just smiled sweetly and her father wrinkled his forehead tightly to keep his eyes from filling up, and the line of mourners — or at least, attenders — moved on.

No one introduced himself as Jon Pear. It was frightening, because surely he would come! His girlfriend's identical twin's funeral? Surely he would come! But perhaps he knew her secret, perhaps he alone could see behind the shaded lenses, and knew she was masquerading. Perhaps he had actually gone through the line already and she had missed it, felt nothing, known nothing.

She saw Scarlett and Van among the mourners, and her heart leaped, wanting to be friends with them, wanting the ordinary delight of their company . . . but they did not come to speak to her. They filed out of the building and back onto the bus without a syllable of condolence.

Is this what memorial services are like? she thought. It can't be! This is so unloving. They seem to be at a spectator sport, not a funeral.

A terrible benediciton seemed to lie over the fate of Mary Lee.

Rest in peace. Nobody will miss you.

Is it a crime, she thought, to use some one

else's funeral as your own? A crime to take over another's room and closet and life and cassettes and telephone number?

There she was at night, in Madrigal's bed, between Madrigal's sheets, and by day, wearing Madrigal's clothing and using Madrigal's lipstick. She chose from Madrigal's earrings, and stared across the bedroom at Madrigal's choice of posters, and sat on Madrigal's side of the dinner table, and answered questions Mother and Father put to Madrigal.

It was the ultimate trespass, and yet, at the same time, the ultimate identical twin-ness.

She hoped for a message, that a twin could talk from beyond death.

But if it was true for any twin, it was not true for them.

The days passed.

The nights ended.

The days returned.

Mother and Father hardly mentioned the dead twin. Mary Lee might never have existed. All sorrow was given to the living, breathing Madrigal. "Are you all right, dear?"

"Are you feeling more like yourself, dear?"

"Shall we go shopping tomorrow, dear, and find some new clothes?"

"Do you feel up to returning to school, dear?"

So she made up the message that her twin would send if she could send, and the message she decided on was this: *MreeLee, you be Madrigal. You be the popular one, who lives at home, and have Mother and Father . . . and Jon Pear.*

To have it all.

Everybody said they wanted it all.

But Mary Lee had it all now, and she did not want it. She wanted to share it with Madrigal, halve it, give it back.

Am I some sort of mental murderer, pushing my sister out of the ski lift with the hands of my hopes? Do I have it all because I asked Madrigal to give me her life?

"We think you need to go back to school in the morning, Madrigal," said her mother.

School. Madrigal's school. Madrigal's boyfriend, of whom she had never even seen a photograph. Yet if Mother and Father had not known, how could Jon Pear?

I can do it, thought Mary Lee. *I can have it all.* "Yes, all right," she said calmly. "I'll go to school tomorrow."

Chapter 6

The drive to the high school was not easy. She was not sure who held the wheel, who shifted the gears, whose eyes checked the rearview mirror and whose foot pressed the accelerator.

I am not dead, Mary Lee reminded herself. Even though I went to my funeral service, and even though the house is a forest of sad little cards about my loss, I am not dead.

She checked to be sure. She had chosen a white shirt, whose lacy front rose and fell as she breathed, and a nearly ankle-length black skirt. Romantic mourning. But over the shirt, a hot pink jacket, because she had gotten a great surprise going through Madrigal's closet. Madrigal twinless — Madrigal on her own — was brilliant and loud. Madrigal had replaced her entire wardrobe. She had discarded the colors and styles of their togetherness.

She felt faintly sick studying this new closet,

this gathering of clothes she must now wear. How quickly, how completely, how vividly, Madrigal had tossed off what they had shared for so long! Whereas Mary Lee had clung obstinately to everything, blocking herself from friendship and pleasure.

A tiny betrayed part of Mary Lee remembered how Madrigal had shrugged when Mary Lee was sent away. She put the memory away, on a mental shelf where she would never have to look at it again.

The Separation had made it all too clear which twin spoke and which one echoed, who strode and who imitated. I must not echo, she thought, for there is no one else to speak first. I must not imitate, for there is no example to follow. I am Madrigal now.

The radio blared. Mary Lee sang along for a few measures to be sure that she still had a voice, was still a person. She drove into the student parking lot only to realize that she did not know where Madrigal's assigned slot was. Fear of being caught turned her hands and spine to cold jelly. She circled the lot and finally chose the Visitors Only slot. Appropriate. Rarely had a student so completely been a Rarely had a student so completely been a visitor.

It was a human fantasy to remain on earth after death. To see what it was like when you no longer existed. See how people had felt about you. Measure the space you left behind.

A thrill of guilt and fear made her breathe faster, less steadily.

She was also, she reminded herself, in love. With Jon Pear. How did a girl in love act? What if she acted wrong? Why on earth had Jon Pear not come to the service? How could he have chosen to stay away from the funeral of the identical twin of the girl he loved?

Were he to discover she was a trick, a substitute, a mere stand-in for the real thing, what would he do? Hate her? Hit her? Expose her? Stomp away from her?

The high school was immense. Its original brick building had graceful white columns and a center dome that glistened in the winter sun. It was now engulfed by several additions.

Engulfed, she thought, and then she was. Drowning in running feet and panicked hearts and screaming silent voices. She shook them away from her, like a Labrador shaking away water.

She looked out the car's windshield and calmed herself by studying the architecture of the school. Each addition was in the style of its time. *I, too, must be in style*, she thought.

Madrigal's style had changed. Mary Lee must do it perfectly, and do it constantly, or her new life would dwindle away.

She tilted the visor down to check herself in the mirror glued to it. The sympathetic hazel eyes looked gently back, and the thick, questioning brows were black velvet against the dark skin.

She was stunning in an outfit meant to catch the eye and keep it.

That was the thing. To keep the eye.

If only she knew whose eye!

He would expect her to know everything, and she knew nothing.

These things she knew: Her stride must be longer; she must possess the halls and floors. Her chin must be higher, and her eyes not linger. Above all, she must never hesitate. Hesitation is weakness.

The moment she entered the first class, her nervousness would be visible to Madrigal's classmates. If she hesitated, if she floundered, they would turn on her like feral dogs at bare ankles.

Even worse — what if nobody suspected, but she failed anyhow? What if she was such a faded copy of Madrigal that people lost interest?

I am Madrigal, she said to herself. And then out loud. "I am Madrigal. I own this school. And I own Jon Pear, whoever he may be. Once

I walk the halls, it will be made clear to me."

She was arriving at ten in the morning. School, of course, began at eight-thirty. But Madrigal would make an entrance, because Madrigal had remained an Event.

If I make mistakes, thought Mary Lee, I'll dip my head, hide the tears behind my tumbling forward hair, explain that death has confused me.

It would not be a lie. Death, especially this death, was quite confusing.

She (whoever she was; at this instant she herself had no idea) held the car handle as she held her two selves. Carefully. Cautiously.

Jon Pear might be watching. It must begin now. Every motion and thought must be Madrigal. She slammed the car door shut at the same moment she took the first step toward the school. Madrigal had connected her Events, whipping from one to the next. Mary Lee stalked up wide marble stairs that led to the front hall, and entered the high school under the frosted glass of the central dome.

"Madrigal," said the principal immediately, scurrying out of his office to take her hands. "Poor poor Madrigal." He was in late middle age, and had lost most of his hair. That hair he had left was combed desperately around his baldness. "We had a Remembrance Service here at the school, of course," said the principal, hanging onto her like a suitor.

A Remembrance Service, thought Mary Lee, almost pleased. I wonder what they said about me. I wonder who spoke. I wonder what poems and prayers they used.

"And the next day," added the principal, "we had a Moment of Silence."

A moment? Mary Lee had died and they gave her a moment? She pulled her hand out of his greasy clasp and wanted to wash with strong soap.

"You're upset, Madrigal," the principal said, putting the same hand on her shoulder, resting it on the hair that lay on her shoulder. Her hair could feel his sweaty palm; she had always had hair like that; hair with a sense of touch. "It is an unusual situation," said the principal, "and none of us can possibly understand the depth of your emotions. I just want you to know that we understand."

"You can hardly do both," she pointed out. It was Madrigal's voice speaking, for Mary Lee would never have ridiculed an adult. "Either you understand or you do not, and in this case, you do not."

He flinched. "Of course," he said quickly. "Of course, Madrigal."

He was afraid of her. His smile stretched in

a queer oval, like a rubber band around spread fingers.

"Walk me to my class," she commanded.

He moved like a good little boy and walked nervously ahead, turning twice to be sure she was still there. The creases in his charcoal suit wrinkled with each kneebend.

The first hurdle was over. Because she did not know, of course, what nor where Madrigal's class was.

She kept her stride long, but measured; setting the pace, allowing the principal to dictate nothing, and yet following him, because she had to. It was an art, and she was good at it. It came from twinship, she supposed, the constant struggle both to lead and to follow.

Struggle. A word she had never used. Had she and Madrigal been involved in a struggle, and only Madrigal had known?

Down the hall, so far away he seemed framed by openings, like a portrait with many mats, was Van. One hour, one dish of ice cream — did that a crush make?

She wanted to run to him, crying, Van, it's me, Mary Lee! The one you flirted with that afternoon, before they told me I had to leave. Van, I don't have Madrigal now, and I need somebody, because nobody can be alone! Please, Van, be mine.

But Van, who must have recognized her, simply stood there, his posture oddly hostile, feet spread, hands out, like a deputy in an old western, ready for the duel.

She caught herself. She was not Mary Lee. Van thought that he had buried Mary Lee. Besides, she was expecting Jon Pear. She must stay within her new life, lest her story dissolve.

The principal halted at an open classroom door, and Mary Lee stopped just before treading on his heels. She forgot Van in the face of so many new problems. For no teacher's name was printed on the door. No subject title was given, no clues passed out.

They walked in. The room was unadorned with equipment. Therefore the subject was not science.

She glanced at a sea of faces, could focus on none of them, and desperately surveyed the front of the room instead. The blackboard was covered with French verbs.

New problems leaped up and assaulted her plans. How good had Madrigal been at French? Where had Madrigal sat? Had she acquired the correct accent? Did she do her homework? Did she get along with the French teacher? Did she come for extra help?

"Madrigal is back," said the principal in a low voice.

"Ah, Madrigal," said the French teacher, clasping her hands prayerfully in front of her flat bosom, *"Je suis tellement désolé."*

How could you be desolate? thought Mary Lee. You didn't even know me.

She remembered, as if she had had an entire hour to relive it, her hour with Van Maxsom.

Is Van *désolé*? Did he think sad thoughts of me during the Moment of Silence? Is he sorry that I am gone? That he cannot even visit my grave, because there is none?

Then why didn't he come up at the service and tell me how sorry he is that my wonderful sister died? Why didn't anybody speak to me? I mean, to Madrigal?

She could have responded to the teacher in French, but did not. "Thank you," she said. There were empty desks. But with whom would Madrigal have sat? Who were her friends?

Not that she and Madrigal had had friends. They had needed no friends. They were each other.

The loss of it was suddenly so immense, so terrible, that she could not maintain control after all, neither of time nor space nor soul. She held everything in her body absolutely still, but it was not protection; the tears still came, soaking her cheeks.

Madrigal! Come back! Please be alive! I love you so!

My twin is cut away. I am severed. The stem without the blossom.

"Poor Maddy!" cried one of the girls. "We're so sorry. What a blow it must have been! And you saw it happen. Poor, poor Maddy."

The class chimed in, sounding rehearsed, each student flinging out a short consolation. "Madrigal, we're so glad you're back," they chorused. "We're so glad you're all right." They did not mention being sorry the dead girl was not all right.

I left no space, thought Mary Lee. Rest in Peace, Mary Lee. Nobody will miss you.

She walked to the back of the room where she sat alone. She wanted to break down on this old marred desk, rip her hair, wear it loose and messy, and scream at these people who could not be bothered to mention her name. She wanted to beat her fists on her chest, rend her clothing, and crash her car.

"*Continuez, Madame,*" she instructed the French teacher.

The French teacher did not call upon her.

Madrigal would have volunteered answers to establish that she was not rocked by catastrophe. But Madrigal's replacement could not find the voice with which she had practiced in the car. And she did not even know for whom she felt the most grief: the dead girl or the living. *Doesn't anybody miss me, too?*

Her heart said to itself: I will be friends with anybody who utters my name. Anybody who says "Poor Mary Lee," I will love that person.

French class drew to a close.

One minute before the bell, she allowed her eyes to drift.

He was there.

Watching her.

It had to be him.

It could be no one else.

Yellow flecks, like gold beneath the waters, glittered in his eyes.

Jon Pear.

His red cheeks grew redder, a rising fever for her. His breathing was too fast, and his wide chest rose and fell like a signal, forcing her own pulse faster. Next to him the other boys, even though they were seniors, were mere reeds, without muscle or brawn. He was a man.

He was so handsome! And yet not handsome at all, but roughly crude, a mix that gave her the same sinking dizziness she'd felt when she entered the school.

Jon Pear, she thought, and the two words of his name seemed precious and perfect. Jon

Pear. And now he's mine. I have it all!

But she said nothing to him. She could think of nothing to say. She knew not one single thing with which to start a conversation.

His smile broke, like thin ice over black water. Like danger.

Mary Lee would have fallen in love with somebody quiet and loving, somebody sweet and endearing. With Van, in fact. But Jon Pear's look was not romantic. Not affectionate, but fierce. Their eyes locked as if in combat.

She was afraid of him. Slowly she made a partial turn away from Jon Pear, pretending to hear the French assignment.

He slowly winked, slowly shifted his own gaze, slowly bestowed upon her the corner of a smile. It was only a wink but it was sickeningly violent. And completely sexy.

Her blood pounded in her ears.

The bell rang.

It startled her heart.

People leaped up. Mary Lee would have leaped up, too, but she was Madrigal. Madrigal, of course, showed no such childish eagerness, but rose gracefully, and stacked her books by size.

He was next to her.

She shivered with extraordinary heat, and felt herself glow.

78

He touched her cheek in an unusual way, dotting it vertically with the very tip of his fingers. She thought the touch would penetrate right into her brain, and give her away. Through the pads of his fingers he would discover somebody else's brain living in that identical flesh.

But it did not happen. "Did you miss our little gifts to each other, Madrigal?" he whispered.

No time to feel safe. For this was a test. She could not know what little gifts he had given her.

Earrings? Madrigal had an enormous collection.

A book of love poems? There had been one by the bed.

A museum scarf? One lay carelessly draped over the chairback.

What to answer?

Between people in love, there could be only one answer.

"I missed everything," she whispered back.

How he laughed! His laugh hurtled over her, a stream in spring, full of melted snow, flooding her. "I knew you would," said Jon Pear. He moved her heavy black hair away from her forehead and kissed the skin beneath.

She trembled violently, for it was her first

kiss. But he had no knowledge of her inexperience. Nothing told him the skin that brushed his lips belonged to Mary Lee.

Courage grew in her. "Come," she said. "Walk me to my next class, Jon Pear."

His eyes were like a tiger's, the pupils vertical. "You want to do it again, don't you," he said to her.

"Of course," she said, heart beating wildly, wondering what *it* was.

"I am Jon Pear," he said softly, as if beginning an incantation. As if he were an emperor reminding his subject who he was. She found it difficult to believe that Madrigal had ever been anybody's subject.

He cupped her two cheeks in his two hands, and she felt eerily possessed. As if she were not a person, but a china souvenir to grace a mantel. An object that could be dusted and cherished. Or thrown against the wall.

Was he toying with her? Had he introduced himself because he knew that she was Mary Lee?

"Jon Pear," she repeated, perfectly matching his emphasis. She was, after all, a twin; she could match with the best.

His shadowy eyes seemed old and distant, having nothing to do with his clear childlike skin. He was a combination of sweet and rough that had neither age nor gender.

Take risks, she said to herself, fly alone in this empty sky. She withdrew from Jon Pear's touch and exited alone from the room.

His emotions were as readable as a twin's — they rushed and flushed with strength. She was amazed at the force of his feelings. He did not like her leaving without his instruction, not one bit.

What if she had ruined it? Should she whirl around and rush back to him, and let him —

She had been correct.

He followed. He begged. He said he needed her. He said he was sorry he had asked for so much so soon.

She could not recall that he had asked for anything.

They had had a secret language, those two. She burned with jealousy, and with grief.

She and Jon Pear were strangely alone in the crowded hall, and yet strangely under observation. She saw in her peripheral vision a hundred students lining the walls, slipping past in single file, or standing at a distance, staring. What a great impression Madrigal and Jon Pear must have made! Why, she and Jon Pear were ringed as by autograph-seeking fans. By people thirsty to see and touch and have inside information.

They're envious, thought Mary Lee, because I have him and they don't.

"Jon Pear," she repeated, tucking his name into her own heart, knowing already that nobody ever called him by just one of his names, or by a nickname.

He took her hand, and it seemed that their hands merged and became one. He looked into her hazel eyes, and his yellow eyes focussed for her as if, from now on, she would see only what Jon Pear saw.

She felt herself rising to meet him, rushing to fall in love with him. It really was a falling sensation, and yet also rising, a tornado of excitement, spinning up and spinning down at the same moment, until she was nothing but a whirl of emotion.

The ring of listening students leaned forward, wanting to overhear. She recognized friends of friends: Geordie, Kip, Kelly, Stephen, Katie, Courtney.

"Shall we choose again?" he said, his voice cracking like ice. Black ice, perhaps, that drivers never saw until it was too late, the car out of control before the driver knew there was trouble.

Her hair, which had always had feelings, prickled beneath his palm, each strand fighting to be free. Whatever choice Jon Pear meant, it was not love, and not nice. Evil soaked his speech.

She wanted to be away from him, to merge and blend with the students along the wall. Instead she was an exhibit at some sort of side show. And what was the show? The choice? What had Jon Pear and Madrigal done on the side, that frightened and drew people?

Fear riddled her, like a shotgun burst in the chest.

Jon Pear laughed again, and this time his laugh was low and musty. It crept beneath things and saw behind things. His gold-stained eyes and white teeth smiled in unison.

Madrigal loved this person? But he is frightening. I am afraid of him.

She would never have used the word boyfriend to describe Jon Pear. He seemed neither boy nor friend.

"I am your twin now," whispered Jon Pear. "At last, you have somebody who truly understands you. A twin of the heart and soul instead of the flesh and blood."

The chorus of classmates on the outskirts of their lives seemed to sigh and hiss.

She looked into the gathering and could no longer recognize faces, could not even recognize features, nor tell noses from mouths from eyes.

Jon Pear came very close. He took her hands away from her face, as if they were his hands; as if he owned them; as if she had them only on loan.

What was he doing?

Again his fingertips dotted her cheeks, but —

What did he —

Jon Pear held a small glass vial beneath her eye. He caught her tears within it, and capped them with a tiny black rubber stopper. The vial, on a heavy gold chain around his neck, fell back against his chest and swung there.

She stepped back from him, staring from the glitter of his yellow eyes to the captured tears. One tear remained caught in her long lashes, and this he touched with a bare finger, transferring the tear to himself. He looked down onto her tear like somebody telling fortunes, and a wild and boyish smile crossed his face.

He ate the tear.

Chapter 7

How safe boarding school seemed now.

How attractive the many miles!

How pleasant the laughing girls who had ignored her.

Madrigal loved this person? thought Mary Lee. On her cheek she could feel dots where Jon Pear's fingertips had touched her skin. Perhaps he had branded her.

He is evil. My sister, my wonderful sister, would never love somebody like this! There is some terrible misunderstanding here.

Just as Mary Lee had always been able to feel her hair, so she could feel her stolen tear. She and the tear were on the inside of the glass vial, slipping on smooth vertical sides, back and forth on the slippery silk vest Jon Pear wore. Why was he dressed like that? Why didn't he wear jeans and a shirt like everybody else? What kind of statement was Jon Pear making?

I am your twin now. Now there was a sick and frightening statement. "I lost my twin, Jon Pear. You cannot replace her. Nobody — nothing — could replace her."

His face shifted. His expressions were a deck of cards being shuffled. He dealt himself to the bottom. Blank and hidden and oddly threatening.

She looked into the crowd where she saw Scarlett, pretty sweet Scarlett. Who needs a boyfriend? Especially this one. I want a girlfriend. A girl to talk to, and weep with, and gossip with, and know me to the bone.

She gave the boy whom Madrigal had loved one more chance. She waited for Jon Pear to express his sorrow. This was the moment for him to say he understood the magnitude of her loss; he knew she must be bleeding as if cut by a guillotine. She would forgive Jon Pear anything if he, too, ached and wept for the lost twin.

But Jon Pear's laughter hung in the air, threatening the standing students. "You don't miss her, Madrigal."

He closed in on her, and she thought he would strangle her, but he kissed her instead, and even though she wanted to run from Jon Pear, she found him so attractive that she also wanted to hurl herself upon him. To kiss until they both died of exhaustion, like a fairy tale in which lovers dance themselves to a frenzied end.

"You don't miss her," he breathed, and his breath was fever hot against her throat. "You got rid of her. Clever you. Everything according to plan. I like that in a woman, Madrigal."

Where his kisses touched, her skin felt stained. She blistered, as if he had the power to cremate her! To turn her, like her sister, into ashes.

"We are the 'us' now, Madrigal. We are the twins. You and I, Madrigal. You didn't need her. You need me."

It seemed to take so much breath to speak. More breath than she could possibly drag into her lungs. She was not going to think about what he had said about planning. He could stain this place with his speech, and he could stain her throat with his kisses, but he was not going to stain her memories of Madrigal. She was going to put him in his place, and that place was far from her. "Twins have to be born," she said. "Twins cannot be made."

But now his big firm hands covered her cheeks, and his fine strong nose tilted down against hers, and his golden eyes stared hypnotically through her own. "I love you," he whispered.

I love you.

There was a no more appealing thought in the world. Jon Pear loved her; she could see that. Even though it was a different beautiful girl he loved. His golden eyes were swimming with emotion, and that emotion was adoration.

As she had been half a person at boarding school, so she half-yearned to have Jon Pear and half-yearned to run away, to put even those two thousand boarding-school miles between herself and his eyes and his vial of tears.

Half is crippled; half cannot quite make decisions. In the moment before she said, *Yes, anything, Jon Pear, yes, you and I will be the twins now*, Scarlett came between them.

Pretty in a soft and doe-eyed way, Scarlett walked forward as if she were actually retreating. She was a deer at the edge of the meadow. Timid, shrinking beauty. "I didn't speak to you at the funeral," said Scarlett. Even her voice shrank, as if she were afraid to get close to Madrigal.

Immediately Mary Lee knew she had hit on it. *They were afraid of her.* Whoever Madrigal had become, her classmates feared her. But how could that be? Madrigal was, after all, just another seventeen-year-old girl! You couldn't be afraid of —

"I miss Mary Lee," said Scarlett. Her sweet

face crumpled in pain. "I think about her all the time. It was a tragedy, Madrigal. You know what I think of you, but still I'm sorry. You must feel pain beyond anything I would, for you were twins."

Scarlett thought so little of Madrigal? Mary Lee tried to catch the meaning, but Jon Pear spoke. "Mary Lee didn't matter," he said carelessly. "Who needed that second reflection in the mirror?" Jon Pear's smile seemed like a passageway to some dark place. He took the ribbon and pins out of her black hair and held the heavy weightlike ropes in his large hands. Then, evilly, he twined the ropes beneath her chin as if he intended to make a knot and hang her on a hook.

She tried to take her hair back, but he kept it, as he had kept the tear.

"I want to put flowers on Mary Lee's grave," said Scarlett, "but I don't know where it is."

She loved Scarlett for being the one to miss Mary Lee. "There is no grave," she admitted, and the loss assaulted her again. Surely it was a terrible omission, to have no place on earth marking the loss of a life. "She is on the wind now. She is part of the air and the sky."

"But that's beautiful!" cried Scarlett. "That sounds just like Mary Lee. Wind and sky."

Van broke through the crowd, ferociously,

as if the student body formed a locked door and he had to clobber people to get through. He approached as if he'd be willing to break wrists to break in.

Jon Pear and Madrigal are an Event, the way Madrigal and I were an Event. I want to be an Event. I do not want to be half, or forgotten, or lost, like boarding school. Jon Pear will make me an Event.

Van left the circle like a warrior with the courage to leave his troops. Alone, he walked toward Jon Pear and Madrigal, as if getting this close was also an Event.

When he looked at Mary Lee, Van sucked in his breath and held it for so long, she had to smile. She forgot Jon Pear, though he still held her hair and her arm. How lovely Scarlett and Van were; how beautiful the friendship of sister and brother. It would be good to have real friends. Mary Lee had drawn a new life, but that didn't mean she had to use every molecule of Madrigal's. She could choose some of her own.

She remembered with a start of surprise that Madrigal had despised Scarlett.

But I'll be friends with her, thought Mary Lee joyfully. Real girlfriends, like other girls. "Scarlett," she said eagerly, "this afternoon would you like to go to the mall with me?"

"No," said Van sharply. "She would not. She has other plans, Madrigal. She always will."

From the gathered, tightening circle of students came another hiss, another murmur, *She always will*.

"How brotherly," said Jon Pear. "Of course, after that unfortunate little episode, Scarlett, I can see how you would need a brother around rather often."

Scarlet paled, pressed her lips together, and lowered her head.

Van stepped between his sister and Jon Pear, and moved her back, as if he were herding her, as if he were her guard dog, and she were a vulnerable lamb. They withdrew into the circle of students, and there they vanished, and Mary Lee could no longer tell one face from another, but instead the students boiled, like water, bubbling and increasing and raising steam.

What little incident? Why did they hold Madrigal responsible?

"There's no need to discuss Mary Lee again," said Jon Pear. He seemed to be addressing the entire school, for his voice soared as if he carried a microphone. "She may not be buried beneath the soil, but Madrigal and I have buried her. Refrain from mentioning Mary Lee again."

People faded and blurred.

Walls left and returned.

Mary Lee found that she was walking beside Jon Pear again, deeply exhausted, as if they had hiked miles together over rugged terrain in difficult weather. "Why did you fall in love with me?" she whispered.

"For your name. Madrigal. Song of the murmuring waters."

She tried to remember what Van looked like but found that she could not. Van, she thought, first syllable of vanish. Perhaps that's all he is, a thing that goes away.

She did not know why she was putting so much value on a mere hour anyway, a mere hour months ago where nothing really had been shared except a snack.

I could be Jon Pear's song of the murmuring waters, she thought.

"And," said Jon Pear, "because you are the twin I have always needed."

She could not snuff out her twinship like a candle. "I'm not your twin, Jon Pear."

Jon Pear's laughter went in and out like tides slapping underground caverns. It passed from good to evil and back.

"Ah, but you are, Madrigal. You and I are twins of the soul."

She was drawn to him like a child to sticky candy, and could not tear herself away.

* * *

Jon Pear walked her to her car.

The school day had been so short! Where had it gone, that collection of classes, acquaintances, and curiosity?

She was filled with thoughts of Jon Pear. They seemed to have multiplied in her, so that there was room for nothing else: his strangeness, his beauty, his familiarity, his ugliness . . . his evil.

She could take neither her mind nor her thoughts off Jon Pear.

Who are you? she thought, for she knew he was nobody ordinary. She wanted knowledge about him. She wanted detail and background. All girls who have crushes on boys want more: they want to see his house, and see his clothes; they want to talk to his friends and see him in sports; they want to read his papers and touch his books and know his life.

She wanted to know which car was his, what he drove, where he was going, but he simply stood waiting for her to drive away.

"Tell me everything," she said to him.

He laughed. It was an ordinary laugh. "You know everything, Madrigal. I didn't leave anything out."

"I want to hear it all again. I love it. I want

you to tell me everything over and over, like bedtime stories."

He smiled, and the smile was like Van's: warm and easy.

He slid the key in the ignition for her, and turned it, and the radio came on with the engine. A fifties rock station. Mary Lee loved that stuff. So soft and easy. But when she danced her shoulders to it, she remembered her dead sister, who would never dance again.

She needed to be alone after all. Scream into the wind and sky, cry out for the sister she had lost. She waited for the tears to come; the tears she wanted, for they would make her feel both better and worse. The only way I will ever feel about Madrigal now, she thought.

No tears came.

Her eyes were dry. Her thoughts were still mainly of Jon Pear, and the dead twin had hardly a sliver, hardly a splinter, of her emotions. And not a single tear. "I can't even cry for her," she said desperately.

"I have your tear," Jon Pear reminded her. His smile increased, blocking roads and mirrors and thought.

She stared at the tiny glass tube on the thick gold chain. "What will you do with it?" she whispered.

His smile grew even larger, like a mushroom

cloud. An explosion. "I like this game, Madrigal," he said. "I'm glad you thought of a new one. We've played the old ones enough."

When she got home, the house seemed more isolated than Mary Lee remembered, the neighborhood more remote, the road less used. Even the house itself looked smaller, its windows blank and dead.

How silent, how sinister, her own driveway felt.

The sky had grown dark early. Shadows were vapor, wafting up from the frozen earth, caressing her legs.

The key trembled in her hand.

She missed boarding school — the chaos and shrieking of hundreds of girls. The lights always on, the radios always playing, the laughter and the arguments always from one room or another.

She tried to picture Madrigal and Jon Pear laughing and arguing, kissing and exchanging gifts.

It was Madrigal's key, of course, because Mary Lee had had to give up everything of her own, and adopt Madrigal's possessions. The key did not go into the lock easily, and when it did go in, would not open the lock.

She stood on the front step, pushing and

turning and clicking and still the door did not open. The shadows behind her crawled up and touched the backs of her legs.

And were they shadows? Or the ghost of Madrigal, trying to come back?

Who was that twin? And who was Jon Pear? What would happen if Jon Pear could read her soul, and imitate her movements, and know her choices the way an identical twin did? Did she want to know Jon Pear the way she once knew Madrigal?

Eventually the key moved and the lock opened. But it was only the key to a piece of architecture, and not the key to any question in her heart.

She could think of nothing and no one but Jon Pear. When she did her nails, when she emptied the dishwasher, when she listened to her parents' chatter, when she watched television . . . hardly a fraction of her participated. The rest was with Jon Pear.

And it was, as he had decreed, like twinship again.

The ordinary world had relatives: parents, brothers, sisters, aunts, uncles, grandparents, cousins. But only twins shared molecules and thoughts. Only twins knew each other's interior.

Now she felt not quite separate from Jon Pear, either.

And completely, hideously, separated from Madrigal.

The evening was heart-quiet.

Mary Lee went silently away from her parents, who had been silently with her. To the bare wood stairs she went — stairs she and an identical person had spent a lifetime running up and down. She went into Madrigal's room.

My room, she thought. I'm Madrigal.

But she was not Madrigal, and she walked in a trespasser. She stood carefully in front of the mirror. Once they had not needed mirrors. She pretended the reflection was her twin. Oh Madrigal, tell me Jon Pear lied! Tell me you had enough love to go around! Tell me you could love this Jon Pear and your love for me was not diminished by it.

But it was difficult to think of Madrigal, for she was entwined with thoughts of Jon Pear.

She took the room apart, inch by inch, studying everything, looking perhaps for an inscription in a book — *love and kisses, Jon Pear*. But there was none.

A treasured greeting card. Scribbled-on, ripped-off notebook paper.

There was none.

Mary Lee was not surprised to find the same

three paperback novels she, too, had purchased, two thousand miles and silence away.

The extraordinary linkage of Madrigal and Mary Lee had often extended to shopping.

Vividly, Mary Lee remembered a morning of rage. Not hers. Madrigal's. In her separate bedroom a year ago, before her own mirror, Mary Lee had stared at herself that morning, bored with the way she did her hair. I'll part it on the side instead, she had decided. The left side. I'll hold it back with my new green barrette.

During her one and only mall expedition with Scarlett, they'd stumbled on a basket piled with gaudy barrettes, marked down from outrageous boutique pricing to affordable leftovers. Mary Lee and Scarlett sorted through every one. Scarlett chose a silver-and-gold braid, while Mary Lee settled on an emerald-green tortoiseshell.

Mary Lee ran downstairs that day to catch up to Madrigal, who was already having breakfast, only to find that Madrigal, too, had suddenly decided to part her hair on the left, and Madrigal, too, at a different store in a different mall with a different shopping partner, had nevertheless found the exact same emerald-green barrette to hold back her hair.

Mary Lee was entranced. Out of an entire

nation of goods! That two sisters in different malls would choose the identical tiny object!

But Madrigal had flung back her head, and *screamed*, a scream of pure wrath, and flung her barrette into the trash. She'd stomped up and down, taking a decade off her age, acting like a toddler in a tantrum. "Why did you have twins?" she screamed at Mother and Father. "I hate sharing my decisions with her! I want to be *one* person! Make her go away!"

How quickly Mary Lee had torn the barrette out of her hair. How swiftly she, too, stomped down, going even further than her twin, crushing the offending barrette beneath the hard sole of the brown loafers — shoes she rarely wore, preferring sneakers. Shoes that Madrigal also rarely wore and, dressing separately that morning, had also chosen.

But later Mary Lee fished Madrigal's barrette out of the trash, washed it off, and kept it. Very soon after that morning, Mother and Father had decided on the boarding school. But even at boarding school, Mary Lee could not bring herself to wear the green barrette. Madrigal would feel it. Two thousand miles away, would get a headache right on the spot where Mary Lee held her hair down with it.

She had meant, over Christmas, and later over the long weekend of Madrigal's visit, to talk about the barrette incident, to see if Madrigal felt better about that stuff now that it had come to an end. But the time had never come to discuss barrettes. *I could wear it now,* she thought, and knew that she never would, for even the ash and wind of Madrigal would hate her for it.

She left Madrigal's room, with its secrets, and went into her own former bedroom. The bed had a comforter, but no sheets and blankets beneath it. The floor had only a carpet. The closet only musty air. The dresser drawers were empty. For her own possessions had not, after all, been shipped back.

Too painful, Mother had said.

We can't bear it, Father had said.

The school agreed to dispose of Mary Lee's things.

Dispose.

It was a garbage word. A trash word.

The possessions of Mary Lee had been disposed of.

She wanted to run down the stairs and fling herself on her parents, let out her pain and anguish. *I made a mistake! Everybody made a mistake! We switched clothes, that's all! And it's me, it's Mary Lee, I'm still here, please be glad, please be glad that I'm the one who lived.*

Yes, she thought, I will do that. I cannot just adopt my sister's life.

Bravely, she left the empty room and headed for her mother and father to tell the truth.

At the top of the stairs she paused, hearing soft conversation between Mother and Father. "I don't miss her," said Father.

"I don't either. But it still hurts so much."

"Of course it hurts," said Father. "But if we must lose a daughter, better it should be that one."

"What kind of parents are we?" said Mother. "And what are we doing now? I'm sure it's another terrible mistake."

"Having twins was the mistake," said Father.

Mary Lee was stabbed through the heart.

She crept back into the room that was not hers, and stood in front of the mirror, trying to grasp the reality that it was only a reflection and never never never again a twin.

Oh, Madrigal! They don't miss me! They think it was a mistake ever to have had me. They wanted only you!

The mirror spoke to her.

Mary Lee shuddered convulsively. Ridiculous. The mirror —

The mirror spoke again.

For a moment she thought it was her sister,

living between the silver and the glass. She even heard her sister's voice, whispering out of the long ago as if, in another life, the twins had lived in a fairy tale. Madrigal had once stood before this very different mirror, murmuring, "Mirror, Mirror on the Wall, Who Is the Fairest of Them All?"

And to Madrigal, the mirror had replied, *There are two of you, exactly the same.*

No! I will not be somebody's double. I will not be interchangeable parts, like something out of a factory! I will not have a twin.

Mary Lee stared at her reflection: the closest she would ever come to seeing her twin again.

When the twins had been Separated, it had been like divorce. Mary Lee got the clean slate and the plane ticket. Madrigal got the new wardrobe and the boyfriend. They had not split the beauty, for their beauty could not be divided.

Madrigal, if we hadn't changed ski jackets, you'd be listening to this mirror. And when you said, "Mirror, Mirror on the Wall, Who Is the Fairest of Them All?" the mirror would say, "You, Madrigal. Only you. Is that what you dreamed of, Madrigal? Being the fairest of them all? Which is something only one can do, and never two?"

The mirror held onto her. "You," spoke the

mirror, its voice silvered and shining.

This was not happening. No. She was reading a children's fairy tale. Remembering a children's story.

"Say it," ordered the mirror.

"Mirror, mirror, on the wall," she whispered. But she didn't care who was the fairest of them all. She didn't even care about being fair. She wanted only to be loved.

"Who is the fairest of them all?" finished the mirror.

The silence was liquid.

"You are," said the mirror. And it laughed, as Jon Pear had laughed, its laugh oozing out like slime from under the silver layer.

Chapter 8

Madrigal is back.

The news whirled like winter winds through the long and heavy corridors of the school. On the second day she was in class, hostility hung in the halls.

The school was overlaid with apprehension. It lay like another textbook on top of everybody's burdens.

Madrigal is back.

Madrigal herself — Mary Lee, that is — was thinking only of Jon Pear.

A good night's sleep had been impossible. But even a bad night's sleep showed her how ridiculous yesterday had been. Of course she had been afraid, but to call her twin's boyfriend evil? Nonsense. Jon Pear, said her mind and heart, Jon Pear Jon Pear Jon Pear.

She was as nervous as a cat on a string, jerking and looking and tying herself in knots.

But Jon Pear was not around.

She found her way to European history without him. This was not a subject Mary Lee had taken at boarding school. It was going to be a challenge, suddenly starting in midwinter. The text was dauntingly thick.

Again Mary Lee sat in the back row, but today she had company — Van. What a pleasure! "It was so nice of Scarlett," she said to Van, "to tell me she was sorry about Madrigal."

Van stared at her.

She'd used the wrong name. She colored deeply. "I mean Mary Lee, of course. I've lost half of myself. I keep forgetting who I am. Because half of me — isn't."

"That's sick," said Van.

"No, that's twins." She tried to imprint the name Madrigal on her tongue. But the name didn't feel like hers. It felt like a summons, as if she were calling Madrigal back. If only she could!

Mary Lee forgot European history.

Grief filled every cell of her body. It was time to weep, to bawl, throw back her head and wail and keen. But it didn't happen. She wept without tears and without sound, a huge and terrible despair for the beloved life that was gone forever.

I have no tears, she thought. Jon Pear took them.

As if he were sitting next to her, she saw the swinging vial of her captured tears. For a moment, she was so fearful she might have been dropped herself into the tube. Her soul encased in glass, fixed by a rubber stopper.

Why can't I cry? she thought. Does Jon Pear have some power over me now that he possesses my tears? Does he own me?

Stop this, she thought. Stop this pitiful absurd train of thought! Some people become deadheads. Some people become glue freaks. Jon Pear is a tear collector. It's a little weird, but Madrigal loved him, so he's lovable.

Van lifted his hand. Mary Lee misunderstood, reached over and clung to it. He took his hand back as she had jerked hers away from the principal. Wishing for harsh soap to scrub off the touch.

Get a grip! thought Mary Lee. Do something, girl, do anything; collect tears, just don't keep having these creepy ideas about people! "That time Scarlett and I went shopping together," she said to Van, and caught herself again, "I mean — she and Mary Lee went shopping — and I caught up to them — that was so much fun. Your sister's a lovely person."

Van was kind, serious, and brotherly, with

all those wonderful traits like medieval knights: gallant and true. She pretended her hour with him was a hundred hours, a week, a hundred weeks. True love.

Van looked at her as searchingly as an explorer hunting for the Northwest passage. "I don't know what you're up to, Madrigal, but don't think for one minute I'll let you near my sister again."

She was getting a pounding headache. She didn't want Van to give her headaches. She was in the mood for love and companionship and laughter.

"And so," said the teacher, "we will split into pairs to discuss the oral presentations you will be giving next month. Madrigal, do you feel up to this? If so, you and Van will work together."

Van gave a strange laugh. His eyes were bright as fever.

Could Van have had a crush on Madrigal? Was he jealous of Jon Pear? So jealous he couldn't even let his sister be friends with her?

If that was true, even Van didn't miss Mary Lee, but had moved right on to Madrigal.

But I could still make it work, she thought. The thing is to bury Mary Lee and really be Madrigal. Take advantage of Van's crush on her. I mean, me. Jon Pear's a little scary. Not my type. I'll drop him. I want to be friends with easy people, like Scarlett and Van.

She said softly, "I'd love to work with Van."

The class turned as one to gape at her. Van's laugh was out loud, and out of bounds. A wild twisting laugh.

Mary Lee wrapped her fingers around the edge of her desk, because she needed something, in this strange world, to hang onto.

Van shoved his desk hard and quick right against hers. He meant to slam her fingers between the desks! Just in time, she yanked her fingers back. The two desks hit hard enough to break bones. She stared at her undamaged hand and then into his eyes.

"Sorry," lied Van, smirking, and she knew — and he knew that she knew — he was only sorry he had not caught her fingers.

Not all the knights of old were gallant. Some were black and evil.

She focused her green eyes on Van, knitting her thick eyebrows above them, trying to find out what was going on.

"You hate me for that day with Mary Lee, don't you, Madrigal?" said Van. "You hate us all. You came into the world a split. A division. The rest of us were born whole, and you'll never forgive us, will you? Well, you have what you want now, Madrigal. You got rid of your sweet sister forever. Leave us alone. Stay with your new twin, Jon Pear. He's your type."

Van's gotten into drugs since I saw him last, she thought.

"Madrigal and I can't come to an agreement on the topic," Van told the teacher. "Would you reassign us?"

Maybe I just need lunch, she thought. Lack of nutrients is making me light-headed and absurd.

"Of course," said the teacher smoothly. "Who will volunteer to work with Madrigal?"

Nobody volunteered.

Nobody moved.

Nobody turned.

No pages flipped. No pencils wrote. No voices spoke.

She was a prisoner in this classroom, with its wall of windows and the straight indifferent backs of people who were not her friends.

Madrigal, whose life she had wanted so much, *had no friends*.

Madrigal had only enemies. People who wanted to crush her fingers between desks.

What have I done? thought Mary Lee.

Van followed her.

If he had been her ghost, he couldn't have stuck closer.

He was staring at her from down the hall,

he was staring at her from the library, he was staring at her in the cafeteria, he was staring at her across the computer carrels.

She wanted him to be the Van of the strawberry sundae, not the Van of the smashed fingers. She looked at her hand. It was unbruised. It had not, after all, been damaged. Only her own nerves were damaging her right now.

Van was studying her. He was so cute. He had that wholesome look, that After-School-TV-Special look, the dear brother who takes care of the dear sister. Perhaps, had he known how, he would have said he was sorry for his behavior in European history.

She smiled at him. Mary Lee's smile. Then of course it was necessary to pull it back, find Madrigal's smile and paste that on instead.

Van stared on, trying to figure her out.

Me, too, Van, thought Mary Lee. I cannot figure out Madrigal's life. If I fail to accomplish even that, what's the point in having it?

At lunch, she joined in the cafeteria line and filled her tray. Food was so satisfying. Boyfriends were not a simple pleasure. But food did not hide itself behind strange actions and strange code words. Food was your friend. Mary Lee loved meals, she loved between meals, thinking about future meals, and remembering past meals.

Pizza day, so she chose extra cheese. She loved pizza, especially the way you dragged the strings of mozzarella through the air, and whipped them around your finger and ate them off your finger, laughing. She took two milks, because pizza induced thirst. She took a green Jell-O, because it had a castle turret of real whipped cream. She emerged from the kitchen tray-filling line and into the cafeteria.

Red tables seating six filled an immense noisy screaming room. Some tables were pushed up against each other. Mary Lee looked into the packed room and knew most of them: people from when she was a twin, and had a person to sit with every moment of her life. People for whom she had been half a set, and who required a name tag to get the right twin.

But no friends.

It was like boarding school. Packed tables for the winners. Spare, empty, distant tables for the losers.

She wanted to fling her pizza tray against the wall and run out of the school. Run out of this life. Where could she sit? Everybody else had a friend!

She saw Scarlett.

Oh, yes, thank you for Scarlett.

She walked swiftly to Scarlett and sat down.

Scarlett was utterly and completely astonished. She exchanged a glance with the other girl seated next to her and both stared at Mary Lee.

I mean Madrigal, she corrected herself quickly.

"Emily," said Scarlett in a strange voice, "I'd like you to meet Madrigal."

"Emily Sherwood," said Emily, without smiling. "Do you have a last name, Madrigal? I have heard you spoken of all day long, but nobody uses your last name."

"She doesn't need one," said Scarlett. "How many Madrigals do you know?"

"Actually, dozens. I've sung in Madrigal choirs for years. You know what your name is, of course. Renaissance song."

Nobody ate. Nobody touched a fork or a cup. They sat very still, watching her, as if they expected her to do something. As if they were braced and ready for the worst.

Mary Lee was crazy for explanations. "Does it seem to you that everybody is hesitating?" she said. "Does it seem to you that everybody is on edge?"

Scarlett and Emily merely looked at her.

A snake sentence slithered through the silent cafeteria. *Madrigal is back.*

And then, unexpectedly, Van was also back.

His handsome thin features were hideously distorted. Van jerked Mary Lee's chair violently backward, dumping her out. Mary Lee nearly hit the floor, but caught herself. "Get away from my sister!" he said angrily.

"I — I thought we were friends," whispered Mary Lee.

The whole cafeteria was watching. Several hundred people were watching. She felt their eyes. *Everybody here knows things I don't.*

"Friends!" said Van contemptuously. "*You?*"

Mary Lee was glad she had not touched the pizza. Glad she had not sipped the milk. Empty, she felt stronger. "What do you want, Van?" Her throat closed. Only a husky remnant of a voice rasped out the sentence.

"I want," said Van, "a ski accident to happen to the right person, Madrigal."

Mary Lee no longer knew what universe she occupied. What language she spoke. Talk to my parents, she thought. They think the ski accident happened to the right person.

"Hush, Van," said Scarlett quickly. "Sit down! Madrigal's just lost her sister."

"The sister they shipped away in the faint hope of keeping her sane," said Van. "The sister they thought they could rescue! The sister they were trying to protect! They figured they'd get poor Mary Lee away from Madrigal before *her* character was ruined, too. But no! Some stupid ski accident has to take the sister who was — "

"Don't make a scene," said Scarlett. "Please, Van."

The words raced through Mary Lee's mind.

Was Van saying that Mother and Father had been attempting to save Mary Lee from her own twin? That there was something so wrong with Madrigal it required hiding Mary Lee on the opposite side of the nation?

Mary Lee was so cold, so frozen, she might actually have been on a mountain, surrounded with snow.

Why had Madrigal come to visit? After saying over and over that she had better things to do, why had Madrigal changed her mind and decided to come to the boarding school? She had not had Mother and Father's permission. She'd arranged it herself. Used the credit cards and gone. Mary Lee thought that was so neat when Madrigal told her: you wonderful brave good dear sister, Mary Lee had thought. Yes! Coming to see your twin no matter what block-ades are thrown in your way. True love!

But had it been . . . true hate?

Jon Pear had actually said — and she had

not listened; he was so scary that not listening was what you did around him — that Madrigal had pulled it off, had destroyed the sister as planned.

I refuse to let these people poison me, thought Mary Lee. My twin sister was perfect. I'm not listening to their terrible words. People who say terrible things are terrible themselves, and I'm writing off Van. That's it, I'm done pretending that hour meant anything. It didn't mean anything to Van, so it doesn't mean anything to me, either.

Then Jon Pear was there.

How had he done it? How had he appeared like this? Why was his schedule not filled with classes like other people?

He and Van were looking at each other like pit bulls eager to rip off each other's flesh. Except that Jon Pear was smiling. "Scenes," said Jon Pear, "seem to be Scarlett's specialty."

Mary Lee didn't want anybody to start anything. How was she supposed to have an ordinary life? "Please! Let's just sit together and have pizza and be friends."

Van stared at her incredulously. "You? Friends? Get real, Madrigal."

"I have lots of friends," she said quickly. "Everybody in French told me how sorry they are for me."

"Everybody in French is afraid of you," said Van.

She knew that. She couldn't keep up the pretense any more. The smiles had been quivers of fear. The sympathy cards that piled up at the house were letters of protection.

I have no friends, she thought.

She wanted to die, the way at boarding school she had wanted to die. Friends were everything, *everything*!

Jon Pear spoke so softly it was not speech, but thought etched with a sharp metal tool upon the opposite brain. "You have me, Madrigal," said Jon Pear. "I am your twin now. Come. We will work on your next gift."

"No!" shouted Van. "We won't let you! Everybody knows what kinds of things you do! There aren't any victims left around here. You can't get away with it again."

"I'm not Madrigal," Mary Lee said, desperate now. There had to be a way out. "I'm Mary Lee."

"You think we'd fall for that?" Van was shaking with rage. "You think we'd believe for one minute that you're sweet Mary Lee? Get out of town, Madrigal. Take your sick boyfriend and go. Nobody would care. Nobody would miss you."

She went.

She could not stand alone, not against an entire school, and besides, Jon Pear cared. He was a friend and, in the end, aren't friends everything?

Chapter 9

I have a boyfriend, thought Mary Lee.

A pillar in a falling world. Somebody to walk with. Somebody who wants to walk with me. Somebody who wants to walk with me only.

Jon Pear seemed to have no classes, no teachers, no school, nothing but the task of moving Madrigal from place to place. He seemed able to stay with her for good.

But is it for good? said the corners of her heart and the depths of her gut. *Or is it for evil?*

His arm lay around her. It was strangely light, as if he were made of aluminum instead of flesh and bone. If she hugged Jon Pear, would she feel ribs and spine? Was he even human?

Mary Lee needed answers.

She began carefully. "Being a twin," she said to Jon Pear, "is like being an occupied country, with an occupying army watching every move. Since I'm not used to being single, I'm trying to understand who Madrigal was just before the accident."

"Who Madrigal *is*," said Jon Pear easily. "It would have been a cute game if Van and Scarlett had believed you were Mary Lee, but they didn't." He smiled at her, a wide shining smile. "And who *you* are, Madrigal, is evil." The smile was happy as sunbeams, yellow dust on warm summer days.

"Not pure evil, of course," he said. His eyes were gold. "I'm pure. You're mixed. But you always surrender to me, because being bad is so much more fun. You're good at bad, Madrigal."

Mary Lee refused to think that. We were identical. I would have known if I had a sister who was good at bad.

Jon Pear drew his finger around Mary Lee's face, as if he were drawing her portrait. As if he could style her personality, and her actions, and even her smile. She knew it was the truth, then, that Madrigal had been good at bad. Would she, Mary Lee, surrender to Jon Pear? Did Mother and Father know? Had they read in Madrigal's heart what Mary Lee hadn't? A turning to evil for the fun of it?

But what was it they did together, Madrigal

and Jon Pear? Whatever it was, it involved victims: Scarlett and others.

"Scarlett," she whispered through thickened tongue and brain, "and the others . . . what . . . ?"

"Who cares about them? They're history, we worked them over." His gold-stained eyes were as impossible to understand as medieval stained glass windows. "Choose another one, Madrigal. It's your turn. I saved your turn when you were offing Mary Lee."

The flecks of gold left his eyes and hung in the air between their faces, like a veil. His eyes, without gold, were black stones at the bottom of some endless shaft.

Mary Lee held her hair behind her head, using her hand for a barrette and thought of Madrigal, flinging away the elegant green ornament as if she were . . . *flinging away her twin.*

Mary Lee wanted to hide. To hide she had to get home, and to get home she had to get away from Jon Pear and from school.

Time to tell Mother and Father who I am, she thought.

How bizarre if they did not believe her, either. What if she had to resort to a laboratory! Genetic blood typing, or something, to prove which twin lived. Prove she was Mary Lee.

"I can't choose now," she said, forcing herself to sound irritable instead of afraid. "It's only my second day back and my heart hurts. I need to be away from all this pressure."

"You love pressure," he snapped.

A shiver raced all the way up her spine into her hair, down between her eyes, and back to her ribs, an all-encompassing shudder.

How do I get out of this? I'll be a victim myself if I'm not careful of Jon Pear. He will hate me for tricking him. He's dangerous. But I can't go on being Madrigal, either. She's dangerous, too.

Jon Pear's eyes tracked the shudder. His shining smile hid behind twitching lips.

"My darling Madrigal," he whispered. "Song of the murmuring waters. We go on, you and I, regardless of your feelings after the fact."

After the fact of what? The — she hated the word; it was a sick ugly horrid word — the *offing* of Mary Lee?

His eyes were boiling. His patience burned off, leaving the real Jon Pear snarling at her. "Pick, Madrigal!" He spit the consonants. "Choose!" He lingered on the vowels. "Who shall it be?"

She had to close her eyes. "Jon Pear, why did you take my tear?"

"What do you mean, why? I love to scare people. People are always scared when you do something they don't understand. Look at you. You were terrified even though you knew perfectly well what I was doing."

"What were you doing?" she said.

Jon Pear was getting really annoyed. He took the gold chain off and dropped it over her head. Her own tear hung beneath her own throat. She jerked off the rubber cap and poured the tear out on the floor. She was being superstitious and stupid, but she hated him wearing her tear. "My sister — " she began.

"Stop using her for an excuse! Once you began loving me, you didn't have room to love anybody else, and you know it. You have a very limited capacity for love, Madrigal."

He kissed her. The kiss was both demanding and giving. She actually enjoyed it, actually wanted more, at the same time she wanted to run.

"You're whiplash," she whispered.

He loved that. He lifted her like a china doll and swung her around. "My darling whiplash," he said, "please choose." He seemed younger than he had, and sweeter.

If I knew the rules to the game, thought Mary Lee, I could play. And if I knew the rules to the game, I could also end it.

He kissed her throat.

She would stop this game as it happened, as she saw the mystery unravel. Perhaps she could be the heroine of this high school! The savior! She'd win those hostile people back as her friends. She'd be the most popular girl in school after all, if she could stop Jon Pear in his tracks. Therefore, she would start in with him. She'd gather facts. Then, cleverly, she'd end whatever charade Jon Pear was playing. "You choose, Jon Pear. I'm too tired."

He doubled over laughing. "All right. We'll cruise the town and pick somebody up. Van has warned everybody here. But there are two private schools and another high school and the Arts and Music High School. We'll go to Arts. Any kid that decides to do nothing but play the oboe all day long is flaky, and they'll go along with flaky suggestions. Once they've gotten started, of course, there's no way out."

Mary Lee felt tough and competent. I will provide the way out, she said to herself. Didn't I survive all by myself at boarding school? I can handle anything.

Jon Pear led her out of the school. Even though she was going to trick him, she felt like a follower, not a leader planning to go in some other direction. Her opposition was melting. She was being steered by him as if she were a wheel. His wheel.

Jon Pear crossed town and found the Arts and Music High School. There, the driveways were so lined by the vertical points of cedar trees, the school was invisible. Only the hedges were real.

The interior of Jon Pear's car was sleek and electronic, stupendously expensive, technologically years ahead of anything Mary Lee had ever driven. He must have a very rich family, thought Mary Lee. She wondered if Madrigal had visited Jon Pear at home. He didn't seem like the kind of person who had a home, or parents, or closets, or breakfast.

Jon Pear frowned. His big lips drew into an odd pout, his golden eyes hooded by his own brows.

The marching band was practicing formations on a field beyond the student parking lots. A single student watched from the pavement. Jeans, jacket, and short hair made it difficult to tell whether it was a boy or a girl.

Jon Pear smiled. "There," he said softly, a hunter spotting a deer. "We've got one."

Mary Lee saw that surrendering to Bad did

not require her to do Bad. It only required that she go along with it. "What will you do?" she asked, sick and fascinated at the same time.

Jon Pear laughed. "What will *we* do?" he corrected her.

Chapter 10

Jon Pear parked, leaving the car without a word. She sat in the passenger seat, knowing that neither she nor that student in jeans should be a passenger of Jon Pear's.

It was a girl, lots of makeup on a gamin face, hazel eyes, and tipped nose. Her legs and tiny feet treated the band's marches like ballet music, and she danced in slow motion as Jon Pear spoke to her.

Again and again, she giggled, tilting her head flirtily, dancing.

Jon Pear was at his handsomest. His golden-certain self gleamed like a trophy before her. When she paused to hug herself against the cold, he whipped off his jacket like her male dance partner and roped her close to him with its empty sleeves. They both laughed, and he leaned down, and she leaned up, and they touched — not lips, but foreheads.

Jon Pear escorted her to the car.

She, too, had surrendered. Whatever he had offered her, she was eager to have.

Mary Lee trembled, but the girl was laughing.

"Hi," she said to Mary Lee, ducking into the backseat. "Jon Pear says you're getting up a party to go into the city. I never go in unless I'm with friends because you know it's so dangerous. But when you're in a group, of course, you're not afraid, so this is really great. I've been noticing Jon Pear around the high school. I don't go to Arts yet, but I keep applying, maybe some semester I'll qualify, but of course right now I'm only a sophomore at the regular high school with you. This is pretty neat, what a great car! I usually don't hang out with seniors. In fact I hardly even know any seniors. My name is Katy, and you're Madrigal, aren't you? I love your name. Jon Pear says it means song of the murmuring waters. Are we just going to party? See a movie? What will we be doing? Who else is going?"

Katy did not seem nervous, but as if babbling was normal for her.

Jon Pear eased his car off the Arts campus. His eyes were icier than the wind, and his smile more cruel.

The car, utterly silent, without the slightest

bump or jostle, moved on like soft butter being spread. At a stoplight, where the car ceased traveling forward so gently, so imperceptibly, that Mary Lee could not even compare it to normal vehicles, she thought: I'm just getting out. There's a McDonald's over there, I'll just use the phone, call Mother and Father, leave Katy and Jon Pear to whatever —

The door handle did not move.

The temperature in Mary Lee's body dropped several degrees. Without attracting any attention she slipped her fingers to the door lock on the window ledge. She could not pull it up.

Jon Pear was smiling broadly. He did not look at Mary Lee. He did not look at Katy in his rearview mirror. He smiled down the road and into the night he had planned.

Van had supposedly "warned" everybody in the high school — but two thousand students attended that high school. Nobody knew "everybody." When people said "everybody," they meant the hundred or so kids they actually knew.

So this is what a victim looks like, thought Mary Lee. *Katy.* "Don't you have to call your parents, Katy?" said Mary Lee.

Now she had Jon Pear's attention? "What are you up to?" he hissed incredulously.

Katy was bouncing eagerly, a ballet dance from the waist up. "Heck no. My parents never care what I'm doing. I mean, they don't even care what they're doing, you know what I mean?"

"I know what you mean," said Jon Pear sympathetically.

Mary Lee didn't. What kind of parents were those?

Jon Pear passed the fast food places: Burger King, Roy Rogers, Arby's, Subway, and Dunkin' Donuts vanished. He passed motels and garages, discount stores, and factories.

He accelerated, and drove upward onto the raised superhighway that led into the depths of the city.

"Jon Pear, this is a limited access road," said Katy. "I mean, like, from this road we sure aren't going to stop at any houses. I thought, you know, lots of people were going to the party. How are you going to pick anybody up? Did you actually mean to get on at the next entrance? Because I know a shortcut if what you want is — "

"We'll meet everybody else there," said Jon Pear.

Who will they be? thought Mary Lee. Who are the other players in this game? If I don't go along with Jon Pear, I won't get answers and be able to stop him . . . but what if I can't stop him? What if Katy and I end up in serious trouble? And neither of our parents will know where we are?

It seemed more and more possible that her identical twin had gone on dates not to dance, not to see movies, not to park the car and kiss . . . but to hurt people.

"I don't want to go after all," said Mary Lee. "Take me back to the school. I have to get my car. Katy, I'll take you home."

"Oh, I don't want to go home," said Katy quickly. "I mean, this is pretty exciting. I don't get to do stuff very often."

Jon Pear's laughter filled the glossy car. He clicked on a CD and turned the volume up high enough to move tectonic plates. Rap. Words of rage and hate blended with screaming instruments.

Seventy-five miles an hour. Impossible to open a door and escape, even if the doors opened. The driver, however, controlled the locks.

The suburbs ended.

The city began.

It was a city whose symphony and museum, fabulous department stores, and famous shops lay in the very center. Ring upon ring of abandoned wrecks of buildings circled the safe part.

The safe part—joke; this was not a city with safe parts—was contained in a very small area. People drove into the city only on the raised highway, keeping themselves a story higher than the human debris below.

It was a place where garbage was permanent and graffiti was vicious. The homeless died in pain, and the drug dealers prowled like packs of animals looking for victims.

Mary Lee did not like to look out the window whenever she went into the city, because the alien world down there was so horrid she could not believe they were citizens of the same country. Guilt and fear cancelled each other out, and she just wanted not to see it, and not to let it see her.

Jon Pear got off the highway.

"Not here," said Mary Lee in alarm.

The road onto which he exited was pockmarked like a disease. Shadows moved of their own accord, and fallen trash crawled with rats.

"Jon Pear, you got off too soon," said Katy nervously. "People never get off the highway here. Get back on! The only safe exit is another mile up. This is a terrible neighborhood, even I know that. Jon Pear, we can't drive here!"

Jon Pear smiled and drove here. He drove very slowly, the way only a big, heavy car with automatic transmission can move: creeping like a flood over flat land. So slowly they could see into the broken windows and falling metal fire escapes, down the trash-barricaded alleys and past the sagging doors of empty buildings.

A gang in leather and chains moved out of the shadows to see what was entering their territory.

"Jon Pear," said Mary Lee, too afraid to look and much too afraid not to look, "what are you doing?"

It was impossible to imagine that human beings lived here. It was another planet . . . as the mind of Jon Pear was another planet.

The gang could have enveloped the car, but perhaps they were too surprised, for they simply watched, and Jon Pear turned the corner.

Here, not even streetlights worked; they were long destroyed. Not even cats prowled. A stripped car lay rusting on the sidewalk. Distant sirens as distant as foreign lands whined.

Jon Pear stopped the car.

What if the car breaks down here? thought Mary Lee.

She tried to picture her sister doing this and could not. Madrigal, to whom beauty and order and perfection mattered?

"You better sit up front with us, Katy," said Jon Pear. "Madrigal, move over closer to me.

Katy, get out of the car and get in front with Madrigal."

"I don't want to get out," said Katy, terrified.

Jon Pear swivelled in the driver's seat. He extended his right arm in a leisurely manner, so it lay over the back of the seat. His golden smile filled his entire face, and he swivelled his head and widened the smile even more.

Katy had no smile whatsoever.

"What do you think we're going to do?" said Jon Pear. "Leave you here?"

There was a soft friendly click, and the locks on the four doors rose, like tiny antennas.

"Come, Katy," said Jon Pear, "come sit in front with us. Just open your door and walk around."

I can't let her do that, thought Mary Lee. He might — he might actually — no. Nobody would do that. But what if he — no. I refuse to believe that —

Katy got out.

Jon Pear, his smile completely intact, as if he had become a wax figure of himself and would gloat for eternity, reached back, shut her door himself, and locked up.

"No," whispered Mary Lee, and she was not saying *no* to Jon Pear, or *no* to the neighborhood, but *no* to Madrigal, who had done this before.

Jon Pear put the car in drive but did not set his foot on the accelerator, so that the car moved of its own accord, only a few miles an hour, and Katy could keep up with them if she ran fast enough.

Katy pounded on the metal of the car. "Stop the car! Let me in! What are you doing? Do you want me to get killed?" She was screaming. Her own screams would bring the gang.

Mary Lee was immobilized. This, then, was the entertainment of her own twin. Evil without vampires, evil without rituals, evil without curses or violence.

The simple and entertaining evil of just driving away.

Katy's face was distorted with terror. Her fingers scrabbled helplessly against the safety glass.

"I love panic," said Jon Pear. "Look what it does to her face."

I should kick him, thought Mary Lee, disable the car, call the police, hit him with the tire iron. "Jon Pear," she said. The words hardly formed in her mouth. Or perhaps her mouth hardly formed words. Everything was wrong with everything. "Stop the car. We have to let Katy back in."

"We never let them back in, Madrigal. Don't be ridiculous."

We never. So her twin had done this more than once and, presumably, once to Scarlett. No wonder Van hated her.

But why hadn't police been called? Why hadn't authorities stopped Jon Pear and Madrigal? If the whole school knew, why weren't people doing anything?

She would have to tell her parents.

But what parents would believe that their sweet beautiful darling daughter had a hobby like this?

No trigger pulled. No match lit. No poisons given.

Just driving away. That was all you had to do. Drive away.

"What did you do to Scarlett?" said Mary Lee.

"Me?" He lowered his eyes. "I beg your pardon. *You* chose Scarlett."

Katy screamed and scrabbled and crawled on the sides of the car.

"And what happened?" said Mary Lee.

"You well know. You orchestrated it."

"Tell me again."

Jon Pear relaxed. "Oh, you just want a bedtime story. You just want to wallow in the details again. Well, she was much more scared than Katy. I like talking about it."

"Talk" was a nice, friendly, folksy word. This was not "talk." This was obscenity.

"Scarlett didn't even run after us. She just folded up on the sidewalk. Then rats came out to investigate. She didn't get bitten or anything, but they walked on her. She went insane for a while, I guess. It was so neat. We followed her block after block, just watching. She was seeing rats everywhere. She ran deeper into the tenements instead of out. She kept screaming 'Help!' As if anybody here would help anybody. They were probably all laughing, too, if they heard over their radios and televisions."

Katy stumbled and fell, leaping up with the strength of terror, trying to climb right up the car. Jon Pear, amused, accelerated. "Don't you love it when they panic so much they aren't human anymore," he said.

Katy was not human anymore. Panic had scraped off everything but the desire to survive.

"That was beautiful. I love fear," whispered Jon Pear. "I love panic."

Jon Pear turned a corner.

A dozen blocks away were the glittering prosperous lights of safe downtown. If Katy kept running, she'd make it. But Mary Lee could not even roll down the window to yell instructions. Jon Pear had sealed the car.

And even if Katy arrived in the safe part, what then? Did she have the money to phone? Would she go to the police? Would she call those parents that didn't care where she was?

"Why didn't the Maxsoms do something to — " she could not say *us*. "I mean, why didn't Scarlett and Van — "

"They never tell," said Jon Pear. "I don't know why. People are ashamed. Victims always think it's their fault. That's one of the neat things about this, don't you think? They blame themselves. They tell half of it, or none of it, or lie about it, or wait months."

He paused, not worrying about traffic, because no one sane would drive here, and looked back to see if Katy was emerging from the pools of dark. She wasn't. Perhaps she was already trapped.

"Old Scarlett was so blown away," said Jon Pear, "that even though a fire truck happened by and found her, she got her story so wrong it was comic. She got the times wrong and the description of the car wrong and the rats wrong. You and I really couldn't have done it! Hysterical. Scarlett set us free. Van's a little irritated, of course. Scarlett spent two weeks in a mental ward, getting rid of rat visions. I found a rat and put it in her locker, and she ended up back in the hospital. The only thing wrong was I wasn't there to see her face when she opened the locker. There's no point in doing this stuff if you don't get to see them panic."

Mary Lee would have preferred to find that Jon Pear had fangs and supernatural skills. But he was just a teenager without a soul or a heart, without a conscience or a care.

And so was my identical twin.

Jon Pear explained himself with the open heart of a lover. "Jon Pear has always been alone," he said, as if Jon Pear were some third party. "Who would have guessed that he'd find a partner?" He held her hand as he drove, and squeezed it affectionately.

Jon Pear swam under the water of evil. It lapped up against Mary Lee, as if she were a pebble on the lake of evil, soon to be covered by a wave of it.

"It's wrong," she said to him.

"Of course it's wrong. That's the fun part." This time he held her in his arms as if about to declare wedding vows. "Oh Madrigal!" he breathed. He drank in her beauty, and Mary Lee saw that he truly was in love.

She would have thought evil people were incapable of love, but she was wrong: Evil could love just as deeply.

For Jon Pear loved Madrigal.

"Oh, Madrigal, I'm so glad Mary Lee is gone out of our lives," said Jon Pear. "Those foolish, friendly, forgiving thoughts she was always cluttering up your mind with are gone forever."

Mary Lee spun out into space, as if she were a black hole, an eternal sorrow. He kissed her and in spite of the horror it was a wonderful kiss, because it was truly full of love. Who would have thought that love could flourish in an evil soul?

"You're just like me," Jon Pear told her. "For you, people are no different from sheep or ants or hamsters. Just breathers, to provide entertainment."

The gold curtain dropped over his eyes.

"And now," said Jon Pear lovingly, opening her door, "I want to see you scared, too."

Chapter 11

I just won't move, she said to herself.

I'll just stand very still, right here in the street.

Nothing can happen to me in the middle of the pavement.

Jon Pear sat within the locked car, the tiny little lights on his dashboard flickering upward under his chin. He was laughing, his mouth open, his white teeth tinted by the lights.

His glittering golden eyes waited for her to panic.

His chest lifted and fell too fast, a panting dog ready to bite.

She could not look at him. He was not human.

Mary Lee looked away, down the street into the total black and up the street where Jon Pear's headlights made queerly yellow shadows. She needed an ally. Somebody to stand with.

This is no different from boarding school, she thought, no different from the cafeteria. All anybody wants in life is somebody to stand with!

Mary Lee called out to Katy, but terror had robbed her of the air to support her voice. Only a mumble came from her mouth. Nobody came to her aid.

A rat, however, came to her feet.

She had not known a rat would be that large, that sure of itself. She had not known its little eyes would fix on hers, making its little rat plans. She had not known its long, hairless tail would be so plump.

The rat grabbed her dangling shoelace in its teeth, its teeth yellowy green. Now the scream Mary Lee had not been able to produce invented itself.

She felt her face change shape and her jaw stretch, she felt her eyes scream along with her mouth, widening and gaping. She heard the terrible sound of her own horror scraping its way out of her lungs.

She kicked. She didn't want even her shoe to touch the rat. She had to get it off her! Get away!

Mary Lee, too, tried to mount the car body, tried to tip the windows down, tried to tear the doors off the hinges — anything — just to get inside, be safe, be civilized.

Jon Pear was delighted.

Bright-eyed, he watched her.

The rat followed.

She choked on her own scream.

How silent was the city. How soundless the rat.

There was no urban din. No radio. No engine. No horn. No bark.

Just the heaving of her own chest, the sucking of her own lungs.

She ran. She had to run. She didn't know if she was running from Jon Pear — sitting all normal and cozy like an ordinary high-school boy waiting for the light to change — or from the rat.

Only the rat followed her.

The street belonged to the rat. She had to leave the street. She had to run faster than the rat. She would go into this building — she would — but no human beings went into this building. She made it up the first step, and up the second, and while her foot was still in midair, reaching for the third, she saw how the doors and windows were solid: blank, with splintered plywood nailed on to make empty boxes of night out of ordinary buildings.

The third step collapsed. Sneaker and sock were slashed as her foot went down. Down into air, down into nothing, down where probably not just rats but also snakes hid! Down with spiders and things that bit and things that chewed.

Mary Lee had not known she possessed as many screams. They came rolling out of her like links on a chain, one after another, huge shining polished screams.

Jon Pear was backing up his car. He was not a good backer. The car veered first to the left and then to the right. She hoped he would crash into some unyielding brick building and total his car, but he wasn't going fast enough for that.

Rolling down his window with the little push button, Jon Pear grinned at her. Loose and easy, like a cheerleader at a game. "Hey, Maddy, what's happening?" He giggled.

Mary Lee thought: My sister Madrigal enjoyed hurting people. Madrigal did this. More than once. She sat in that car with Jon Pear, with the windows up and the doors locked, and she laughed while her face turned green in the light and her victim screamed among the rats.

My twin.

Katy staggered around the corner. Her eyes

were unnaturally wide. Her hands were filthy and also her kneecaps; she'd fallen in a gutter and the trash had stuck to her.

Jon Pear vaulted out of the car. He escorted Katy to the car like a boyfriend privileged to have such a pretty date for the prom.

"Jon Pear," whispered Mary Lee. "Jon Pear, I can't get my foot out. I'm stuck."

"Dear, dear," said Jon Pear, tucking Katy into the front passenger seat, and gently fastening her seatbelt, and gently closing her door. Jon Pear waved at Mary Lee. "Bye, bye, Madrigal," he said softly, blowing her a kiss.

He strolled around the car to get in and drive away.

Lock him out, Katy! thought Mary Lee. Lock Jon Pear out in the street and drive away! I don't care what happens to me as long as Jon Pear gets his! Lock the doors, Katy.

Katy scrunched against the door, clinging to herself and the armrest.

Mary Lee's screams were all used up now, tired and pointless, and the tears began.

Jon Pear scared Madrigal so much that my sister had to participate, thought Mary Lee. My sister didn't really want to do this. Jon Pear forced her . . .

No. The sister who visited her at boarding school hadn't been afraid of her boyfriend. The thought of Jon Pear had brought only smiles to Madrigal's face.

No wonder Van hates me, thought Mary Lee. No wonder Scarlett is afraid of me.

Jon Pear rested on the back of the car, like a horse trainer lounging against the fence.

She knew what he wanted. He wanted her to beg. Say please, say the magic word.

He wanted power.

He wanted proof that he could give fear and take away fear.

He could start panic and take away panic.

I will stop him, she thought, I will end him. I will never never never let Jon Pear hurt anybody else again!

"Please, Jon Pear," she begged. "Please don't leave me here."

He stomped down on the broken step, breaking it more, and giving her room to pull her foot out. He helped her into the backseat. Very gentlemanly. When she sagged down onto the leather, the soft-as-butter leather, the warm once-alive leather, she felt safe and civilized again.

Jon Pear actually said thank you to Mary Lee when he started the car. "That was great, Madrigal," he said. "You were great. You were as scared as any of them. Because you knew

I'd really drive away. You really knew what to be scared of."

Jon Pear laughed happily and changed radio stations.

"Wasn't that a high, Katy?" said Jon Pear. He flashed his marvelous smile at her. The smile had a life and character of its own. He was the sponsor of the smile, but it wasn't his. He'd just bought it somewhere. "Weren't you thrilled, Katy? There's nothing like having your life in danger."

Katy burst into tears.

They reached a red light in the center of downtown, ten blocks and a million emotional miles from where he had dumped Katy. Theater patrons bustled in their finery, and the late-night restaurant crowd rustled in and out bright-lit doors. The music of pianos and small bands spilled out onto the friendly sidewalks.

Jon Pear took Katy's hands away from her face as if those were his own, as if Katy had them on loan. Her face was stricken and tear-stained. He chose a tear, lifting it carefully with a bare finger. He looked down onto the tear like somebody telling fortunes, and a wild and boyish smile crossed his face.

He ate the tear.

Mary Lee made herself think of good things. Of parents and warmth, of sunshine and autumn leaves, of laughter and sharing. Once she would also have thought of twins, but there was no beauty in that thought now.

"Tears are the soul," said Jon Pear. "Tears are pain."

No, thought Mary Lee, tears are just proof. Just a weird creepy way of showing that you made somebody cry.

She saw there was just something animal about Jon Pear; he was closer to the rat. He was a boy, a high school boy, but a wilding. He was so handsome, so well-packaged! It was hard to tell, beneath the good clothing and the great hair, the shining smile and the fine speech, that he was less, not more.

Subhuman, she thought. That's what it is.

How much, she thought, as Jon Pear's car moved through the city and got back on the highway, how much did Mother and Father know? They knew I was in danger. Did they know exactly what Madrigal was up to? Did somebody's parents call them? Did Madrigal brag? Did they follow her?

Now the two thousand miles her mother and father had chosen seemed like a fine gift. If only it had worked! Mary Lee would have been happier to be lonely and confused all her life, than to know what kind of person Madrigal had really been.

I have to be sure Mother and Father know that I'm really Mary Lee. We have to bury Madrigal, and we have to bury her deep and forever.

And Jon Pear . . . how do we bury Jon Pear?

Mary Lee made plan after plan. But nothing would really work. Jon Pear would slide out of whatever came and wait a while and then — here or elsewhere — start up again.

Katy and I will go to the police, she thought. The simple solution is always best. We'll tell the authorities and have Jon Pear imprisoned.

But Jon Pear had been here before. How clever he was! In moments, he had Katy giggling to please him. He had Katy admitting that the night had been a real high. He had Katy pressing her lips together in a one-person kiss, listening to a hint that Jon Pear might ask her out again one day.

It chilled Mary Lee more than the rat.

Katy was cooperating.

Katy wouldn't tell a soul.

So there would be no police to stop Jon Pear. No principal, no parent, no passerby.

Only Mary Lee.

They took Katy home. She actually said thank-you after she said good-bye. Jon Pear laughed all the way to the high school.

How Mary Lee yearned to be in her own car! Doors locked, wheels pointed toward the safety of home.

There had evidently been some event at the school, for late as it was, people were pouring out of the building, laughing, cheering, and thrusting fists of victory into the air. Boys were whapping each other on the back, and girls were hopping up and down with delight.

How nice to enjoy a sport like basketball, where the worst that can happen is you lose. Whereas Madrigal's sport . . .

"Jon Pear," said Mary Lee, "we're not going to hurt anybody again. This hobby is over."

It startled him. "What are you trying to pull?" said Jon Pear suspiciously.

"This is truly bad! You have to stop being so rotten."

Jon Pear laughed. "Too much fun. You should have seen your face, Madrigal. You were so scared. You were jelly. You were panic. You were gone, girl. And everybody is jealous of me. I do what I want. They want to, too, but they're timid, see. My plan is to get them all. We'll have a whole school of people who will do anything to anybody."

"You will not! They won't cooperate with you. This school is full of good people! Kind, generous, decent people."

He was skeptical. "Name one."

It was easy to name one. Easy to name two. Scarlett and Van were kind, generous, decent people."

"Van," she told Jon Pear. Just uttering Van's name made her feel better. "Van is a good person."

She had made a mistake.

A huge and serious mistake.

Everything about Jon Pear darkened and deepened. He moved back from her, and she saw, for a splintered second, the creature that was beneath his skin. A creature with no compassion, no humanity. A soul as empty as the glass vial in which he had dropped her tear.

"You like him," said Jon Pear. He was truly shocked. *"You like Van!"*

She had forgotten that Jon Pear loved Madrigal. Trusted Madrigal. Confided in her.

She had betrayed Jon Pear. And in so doing, had betrayed Van. For Jon Pear, who had simply wanted entertainment, now had a greater motive.

The desire to hurt Van flared on Jon Pear like sunspots. It blinded Mary Lee, as if looking Jon Pear's way required special lenses.

Jon Pear got out of his car and searched the crowds.

Coming through the high school door were Van and Scarlett.

"Why, Van," said Jon Pear, his smile growing.

"Why, Van," said Jon Pear, gliding forward like a creature of the water, without legs, without steps.

Chapter 12

Van stepped in front of Scarlett.

As if standing first in line ever saved the second person.

But Mary Lee loved him for it. Once I was that close to my sister, she thought. Once Madrigal and I trusted each other and looked out for each other.

When the twins were little, Mother used to say, they'd fall asleep at the exact same moment, the rhythm of their breathing identical. They would eat their cereal in synchrony, each little right hand moving a spoon as the other did. They would run to the schoolbus stop, each skip timed like a choreographed dance number.

Where did you go, Madrigal? asked Mary Lee.

But she could not spend time on a ruined sister. She had to move on. "Leave Van and Scarlett alone," said Mary Lee. Her voice felt old, as if she had dug it out of some dusty history text.

Jon Pear, of course, never even looked at her, but continued to advance upon Van.

She stepped between them.

"Madrigal, this is my game," said Jon Pear, never lowering his eyes to hers.

"These are people. They aren't a game." She stepped in front of him again.

He was incredulous. Nobody blocked the path of Jon Pear. "What is going on here?" demanded Jon Pear. "Who do you think you are?" His voice was no longer water rippling over the rocks. It was the rock itself, sharp. "I do anything I want."

"No."

"Madrigal," said Jon Pear. "You're making me angry, Madrigal."

She shrugged. The pretense of being Madrigal felt as if it had lasted for weeks. Drained her like a wasting disease.

Jon Pear wanted to shove her away. She could feel his yearning to push her trembling on the other side of his own extended hand. He controlled himself, but just barely. The violence in Jon Pear was growing. She felt as if she were standing over a geographic fault line.

Who is Jon Pear? she thought, staring at his fury.

She knew nothing of his history and nothing of his present. Did not know his address. Did not have his phone number. Jon Pear had never mentioned parents — never quoted them, referred to them, groaned about their rules, hoped for their approval. He had mentioned no sisters or brothers. No dogs, no bedroom, no possession had been worth describing. He seemed to play no sport and, although he attended classes, he seemed not to be enrolled in them.

He was just there.

"If your plan, Madrigal," said Van quietly, "is to pretend you're on our side, so you can get us to go along with you, or divide us, you need to know we can see through you. You're as sick as Jon Pear is."

She wanted desperately to have Van know who she really was.

"It won't work, Madrigal," said Van. "We've played too many of your games. We're not playing this time. We're going to our car. You are not getting near us. Neither of you. You are not to touch us, nor speak to us. Ever again."

Mary Lee's heart was breaking. She flushed in shame, her olive skin turning hot and beautiful.

Jon Pear said, "Madrigal?" She could not tell whether he shook from rage or adoration.

Van and Scarlett took a single stride toward their car, but Jon Pear leaped between them and safety. He spoke to Madrigal, but he stared into the eyes of Van and Scarlett.

"Remember the day we saw somebody drowning, Madrigal?" said Jon Pear. "Remember how you and I stood on the shore and watched? Remember how bright and gaudy the autumn leaves were, drifting down on the water where he went under? Remember how he came to the surface again and signalled us? He knew we were there, Madrigal."

The miasma of his evil spread like a fishnet. Mary Lee tried to step away, but his voice caught her. She was prisoner of his voice the way she had been prisoner of the broken step.

"The last time he came up, and didn't have enough strength to call out to us, we waved at him." Jon Pear's eyes glittered like diamonds. "You and I, Madrigal. Remember what fun that was, when he went down? He knew we could have done something. And he knew we wouldn't. That's the most fun," Jon Pear confided. "When you *could* do something, but you don't. And they realize it, the victims. They know you chose to let them drown."

Scarlett was weeping.

Van continued to appear preppy and perfect,

athletic and interesting. But his complexion drained of color, and beneath his tan he was gray. As gray as the skies and the heart that had accompanied Mary Lee on her plane trips.

Mary Lee, too, struggled for air she would never find and reached out with frozen fingers to haul herself to safety, and found only a maple leaf. In a voice that had no sound, only horror, she said, *My sister did that?*

Her knees buckled. Half-fainting, Mary Lee ended not unconscious but kneeling in front of Jon Pear, as if begging for mercy.

"I don't do mercy," said Jon Pear. "I don't do anything I could go to jail for, either. I just stand there. Watching. What happens, happens. I love watching it."

She felt herself folding, growing smaller and smaller. She had nothing inside now but agony. What he was was bad. Not a mirage, not a ghost, not a vampire, but a completely bad person. And either Madrigal had been born the same, or he had taught her to be the same.

"And you do, too, Madrigal. Don't pretend now that you didn't enjoy it as much as I did. Don't try to get Van Maxsom back by pretending you're really a nice person. You're Madrigal, who stands laughing while people die." He smiled a real smile, the smile of a person who found life satisfying.

"I will do nothing with you, Jon Pear!" she shouted. "I will stop you."

How he laughed. His eyes bright. "Nothing stops me. Least of all you, Madrigal! I'll have whatever victim I want. Including you, if I want you."

In the parking lot that Mary Lee had thought empty, students appeared. They formed a distant circle, silent and watching.

"Ah, this is what I like," said Jon Pear. "A larger audience."

She knew them. Geordie, Kip, Stephen, Rog, Kelly, Courtney, Nate . . . and Katy.

Jon Pear's voice like a satin wedding gown, tempting her down a terrible aisle. "Join me, Madrigal. You and I are twins now, remember. The perfect match."

"No, Jon Pear. Never."

"I own you, Madrigal. I know everything you ever did. I even know you murdered your own sister. Mary Lee was far away but she was still there. You couldn't stand it! You couldn't stand those soft little thoughts of hers wafting home, you couldn't stand that whimpering — *come visit me.* You decided miles weren't enough. You wanted her completely and forever gone."

She spread her legs for balance, and gripped her waist with her two hands for courage. "I am not Madrigal. I do not know what Madrigal had in mind for Mary Lee, but nothing happened to Mary Lee. It happened to Madrigal herself. The body was identified by a ski suit and I, Mary Lee, took advantage. I thought she had the better life, and I thought I wanted her life. Now I see that Madrigal's life was ugly and barren and cruel. And you, too, Jon Pear. You are ugly and barren and cruel. And I will stop you."

The night air was less cold. The wind was more quiet.

"*You* are Mary Lee?" whispered Scarlett.

"She is not!" shouted Jon Pear. He jumped up and down, as if trying to crush the opposition under his feet. "I know everything, and I would have known."

Mary Lee folded her arms across her heart. Either the memory of her twin or the violence of Jon Pear was going to destroy her if she didn't keep a very tight hold. "You know very little, Jon Pear. You know nothing of love. You corrupted Madrigal, but you will not have me."

"You are *Madrigal*!"

"I am Mary Lee."

"Impossible! Nothing fools me. *I would have known*." He clung to the little vial of tears, and

Mary Lee saw suddenly that it was for his sake he had the gold chain and the talisman: It made him feel bigger and better.

She grabbed the chain and jerked it hard, snapping it against the back of Jon Pear's own neck, and she threw it into the weeds where it belonged.

There was silence.

There was darkness.

There was astonishment.

Scarlett whispered, "You *are* Mary Lee!" She pivoted slowly, creeping around behind the safety of her brother, hardly daring to believe.

"I'm sorry." Mary Lee was weeping. "Oh, Scarlett, for all the things my sister did, I'm sorry. I didn't know! I knew some other Madrigal. I don't know who this one was, that Madrigal who hurt everybody and liked it."

Scarlett placed a gentle kiss on Mary Lee's cheek. It was unbearably similar to the kiss of twins. "We forgive you for what Madrigal was, and what she did."

Mary Lee left Jon Pear standing alone. She left him humiliated and tricked. She left after calling him ugly. She stood with Van and Scarlett, with Kip and Geordie, Courtney and Nate.

No one can bear to be left standing alone and friendless.

No one can bear to see a circle of people closing in on him.

The worse kind of person you are, the more you need other people. You have to brag. You have to show off. You have to swagger.

Jon Pear would show them.

He would have something to swagger about.

Chapter 13

As if they had been in a VCR clicked to PAUSE, they now clicked to PLAY.

People moved back to their cars. Chatter and laughter returned. Tonight's athletic event was over; now they must remind each other of the next one, and promise to be there, and to win.

"Winter Sleigh Day is Saturday," they called to each other.

"I'm in the relay race," Stephen said. "What are you doing?"

"I'm selling T-shirts," said Kelly.

"I'm selling hot chocolate," said Courtney.

"I'm renting ice skates," said Rog.

Van and Scarlett walked Mary Lee to her car. Van opened the door for her, and checked to see that the other doors were locked, and waited until she had her key out. "I'm stunned," he said. "I have to admit — I only half-believe you, Mary Lee. Madrigal, you see, was so crafty. She could fool anybody."

"She fooled me," said Mary Lee.

Scarlett said, giving a great gift to Mary Lee, "I don't believe for one minute that Madrigal was going to hurt you when she went to visit. That's typical Jon Pear. He turns a perfectly nice visit to a sister into something evil and violent. I'm sure Madrigal really missed you."

Van looked at his sister. His eyes were flat and his mouth was tight. He believed Madrigal had planned to hurt her sister. He had no trouble believing it at all.

What he had trouble believing was that Madrigal didn't pull it off — that it was Mary Lee who had survived.

Like photographic negatives, in the half-illumination of half-working parking-lot lights, students in cars were ghosts on black. Muffled, their engines began. Slowly, nosing forward like migrating herds, they found the exits and drove away.

Van and Scarlett went to their car.

Mary Lee turned the key in her engine.

Van and Scarlett slammed their own doors and locked them.

Mary Lee's key turned, but her engine didn't.

Van and Scarlett started up and drove away.

Mary Lee tried the key again, and the engine was silent, and again, and the engine was silent, and —

Jon Pear slid into the passenger seat.

"I locked the door!" she said.

He laughed. "I have a key, of course. And I took the precaution of disabling your car, of course. Wave good-bye to your little friends, Mary Lee."

But her little friends were gone, nothing but red rear lights vanishing down the road. The last parting student waved good-bye. Did that person know? Did that driver see who had gotten into the car with her? Was that person doing for a hobby exactly what Madrigal and Jon Pear had done — committing the sin of just driving away?

"Winter Sleigh Day," said Jon Pear meditatively. "Let's spell that differently, Mary Lee. Winter Slay Day." His smile was back. "Whom shall we slay, my new little twin?" His fingers closed over Mary Lee's wrist.

"So you are really Mary Lee." He shook his head. "Fascinating. Madrigal tried to talk back to me once, too."

"She did?" Mary Lee felt a thread of hope for her sister.

"You are braver than she is. You're trying a second time."

I am braver than Madrigal?

"But it won't work. I will make you my twin just the way I made Madrigal my twin. You and I will be twins in evil."

"Never! Anyway, Jon Pear, you're not evil. You're ordinary. You're just mean and low. You're just ugly and pointless. The world has lots of people like you."

Jon Pear was furious. What could be a greater insult than being called ordinary? "I am evil," he told her. He tilted her chin up as if to kiss her lips, but kept tilting as if to snap her neck. "And you tried it, Mary Lee. You were a passenger in the car that put old Katy out in the street."

"I didn't know what was going to happen," she said.

Jon Pear laughed. His laughter rose like smoky pollution from some ancient factory. "You knew something bad was going to happen, and you wanted to see what it was. Don't lie, Mary Lee. But even if you didn't lie, you're still caught. See, once you go bad, you stay bad. You get only one chance. You don't get to say, 'Oh, let's not count this, I'm sorry now, I want to be nice again.' "

"Yes, you can. You can say you're sorry." She wondered what he was going to do to her. He was stronger. He could run faster.

"People love to say they're sorry," he agreed, "and maybe somebody somewhere gives you points for it. But you stay bad, whether you're sorry or not."

There was a sort of purity to Jon Pear. Weren't most people a mixture? Didn't most people, no matter how ugly, have some redeeming quality? Jon Pear was scum, acid.

"How did you disable my car?" she said sharply.

"Oh, right, I'm going to tell you so you can do it to mine." He snorted.

How strange, she thought. It never occurred to me to do it to his, I just wanted to change the subject and maybe even figure out how to get it going again.

"I may have been fooled by a change of clothing, Mary Lee," whispered Jon Pear, and the whisper whistled through the silent frightened night. "But you! You were fooled by Madrigal's entire life."

"Not her entire life," said Mary Lee. "Some of our lives — most of our lives — Madrigal was good."

He snorted. "Madrigal was born bad and got worse. Madrigal hated being a twin. She hated you for flirting with Van that day and she hated you for going to the mall with Scarlett. She hated you for looking the same and sounding the same and acting the same as her. She thought boarding school would be enough, but it wasn't. You were still an aura in the house. Your mother and father still missed you. Your room was still there. She could feel your messages. How you were lonely and scared. Of course, she was glad about that, but she hated it that you still had a thought wave to her."

It was just as well that Mary Lee did not still have a thought wave to her twin. Don't tell me her plans for that visit, thought Mary Lee. Don't give me any details about what Madrigal said she'd do to me.

"Winter Sleigh Day," said Jon Pear. "What is it, anyway?"

Beyond the tennis courts and the big oval track, beyond the stand of pine trees that bordered the school campus, a charming lake emptied into a wild white-water river. Winter Sleigh Day used it all: courts, track, trees, lake, and river. It was a day of merrymaking, the highlight of the season, the most fun and the most friendly.

An idea came to Mary Lee.

"Madrigal and I," said Mary Lee, "always loved Winter Sleigh Day. We wore matching purple-velvet snowsuits when we were little, and Mother curled our hair out around the white trim of our hoods, and we would make maple sugar candy on the snow, and fly down the hill on the toboggan."

"Spare me the infant memories," said Jon Pear. "The past does not interest me unless I am in it."

Mary Lee said, "You must have been in it somewhere. How did you get here? Where did you come from?"

Jon Pear laughed without sound. "My parents are boring. Stupid. Dull. My whole life would be boring stupid and dull, but I decided to have fun. And I'm going to have fun, Mary Lee, and I'm going to have fun with you."

She wet her lips in spite of the fact that Jon Pear would see her anxiety, and use it against her. "Winter Sleigh Day is such a pretty holiday." She closed her eyes and spoke from the darkness. "They have ice carving and snowman contests. They bring in sled dogs. Ice skating and cross-country skiing are competitive events, and there are also silly events, like snowball wars and icicle eating. So no disrupting Winter Sleigh Day, Jon Pear. It's an important day. You need to confine your silly little pranks to school days. No fooling around on Winter Sleigh Day."

"I don't fool around!" said Jon Pear. He muttered to himself. "Pranks!"

"Childish," said Mary Lee. "You're just frustrated. Now, I want you to make a real effort to act more adult. You're not very mature, and if you just try hard, Jon Pear, you can — "

"I can see why Madrigal hated you," said Jon Pear. "You're a lecturing frumpy little middle-aged — "

"I'm just trying to help, Jon Pear. Have you thought of counseling? Well, we'll save that for another day, when you're not so moody. Saturday is Winter Sleigh Day, and you absolutely must not do anything naughty."

"Naughty!" exploded Jon Pear.

"Furthermore, if you were really a man, and had any abilities of your own — "

He wanted to hit her. Every muscle in him gathered for striking. Mary Lee flinched, expecting pain.

But he did nothing. "I don't do violence," said Jon Pear very softly. "I just watch it. I let it happen. So I won't hurt you with my fists, Mary Lee. But I will use Winter Sleigh Day, since it has such a perfect name. Winter Slay Day." Jon Pear was night fog, a wet clinging blanket of evil.

"Do anything you want next week in school," said Mary Lee, all prissy, "but promise me you won't touch Winter Sleigh Day."

"I don't make promises," said Jon Pear, "and if I did, do you really think I would keep them?"

Jon Pear laughed. He got out of the car and unhooked the hood. From his pocket he produced something small and round, which she couldn't see very well through the crack, and screwed it back on. He let go of the hood, and it slammed itself down.

The engine started.

He stepped back so she couldn't just run him over, leaving him in the student parking lot.

"We'll have a contest, you and me, Mary Lee. Welcome to my playground. There are no rules. There is no such thing as fair play. I don't give warnings. I will win."

When she got home, Mother and Father were waiting up for her. They were frightened. They were dressed in jackets and gloves to go out after her, search for her — but they hadn't. Perhaps they knew better. Perhaps they had tried to find Madrigal before — and regretted it.

She went straight to the truth.

"There's something I have to tell you. I'm Mary Lee, not Madrigal. When she was killed, everybody thought it was me. Just the ski suit. That was all anybody based it on. And I let them. I wanted Madrigal's life. Madrigal had you! She had home, and everything I missed so much. So I stepped into her clothing and her bedroom and her life, even her boyfriend and her classes. But I'm sorry now. Madrigal didn't have a life that I want."

She had not surprised them. She saw that they knew; had known from the first. "Mother?" she said shakily. "Father?"

They hugged her swiftly and encompassed her with their love.

"You knew?" she cried.

"Of course we knew," said Mother softly. "Right away. What we did not know was what to do next. We were afraid. Parents should not be afraid."

"Sweetie," said her father, "I don't know what you found out about Madrigal. I don't know what you ever knew. There was something very wrong with your sister. There always had been. She was a scary little girl. She didn't take it out on you, and we thought you were her lifeline to being good. We thought she would outgrow the things she did, and be more like you; be nice. Really nice, not just nice to get something she wanted."

"But it got worse," said Mother. "Each year, she was scarier and scarier. Angry. Mostly she was very very angry. And after a long time, we realized she was angry at you, her twin! Angry that you existed. Angry that she shared her beautiful looks with you."

"Madrigal would stand in front of the mirror," said Mother, "and like a demented queen in a fairy tale, cry, 'Mirror Mirror on the Wall, Who Is the Fairest of Them All?' Then she would be enraged because she wasn't. There was a pair of fairest."

"When your back was turned, Mary Lee," Father said, "she would look at you with such hatred, we trembled. We tried to talk to her about it, and she had her own solution: separate the two of you. So we did."

Did Madrigal always feel that way, wondered Mary Lee, or did it happen over the years? Did Jon Pear come first or during or after?

Oh, Madrigal! I didn't want to be the fairest of them all. I wanted us both to be the fairest of them all! We could have done it. You didn't need to throw us away.

"We failed you," said her father.

"Yes, you did!" cried Mary Lee. "Why did you ship me away? Why didn't you send Madrigal away?"

"Where would we have sent her? Who would have taken her? Besides, we thought we could turn her around. We thought when we had just one daughter at home, and we could concentrate on her, that we could make her good."

"It just gave her more space to be bad in,"

said Mother. "It was a terrible mistake. I go back over her life all the time, trying to see where the first mistake was, and the second, and the third. But I don't find them. All I find are two little girls I loved so much."

"Why did you let me be Madrigal?" she said. She was angry herself. She wanted parents who didn't make such big mistakes. Parents who could tell what was going to happen instead of going all the wrong ways.

"We knew you wouldn't behave like Madrigal. We knew you'd be good. You wanted her life so much. We should have said, 'Mary Lee, forget it. This is Madrigal who died.' But — we were so shaken up, we were so flustered, it was all so horrible — and we let it happen. We just stood there and let it happen."

Mary Lee knew the real horror then. The worst, absolutely worst thing, is to see something wrong, and then just stand there and let it happen.

I've seen something wrong, thought Mary Lee, and its name is Jon Pear, and I'm not going to let him happen again.

The reunion with her parents lasted long into the night, but at last she was in her room; Madrigal's room. The day had lasted a generation.

The mirror was dusty.

"I'm mad at you, Madrigal," she said, as if her reflection were the twin who had been her reflection. "You knew better. I don't care how powerful or how exciting Jon Pear was. You could have chosen not to be a part of it. *How could you do that?* When you and I were part and share of each other, how could you choose evil over good?"

There was no message, for there was no Madrigal.

"Madrigal," she whispered. She touched the mirror, as a thousand times a thousand she had touched her real living twin. "I forgive you. You are still my twin. My beloved twin. Still my beloved sister. You are still half of me, and I am still half of you."

The glass turned warm at her touch, alive and full of hope. *"I still love you, Madrigal."*

Mary Lee straightened her shoulders. "Rest in peace, Madrigal. I am Mary Lee and I will beat Jon Pear."

Chapter 14

The marching band gathered between the track oval and the lake. Brass players warmed their mouthpieces, huffing constantly. Third-graders in crayon-colored ski suits got ready for their ice-skating relay races.

Fourth-graders drank hot chocolate, while fifth-graders prepared maple-sugar-on-snow candy. The big boys got ready for snow wrestling. Forts for the snowball war were being built. The log cabin with the huge stone fireplace was the only warm spot at Sleigh Day, and children raced in to dry their mittens and raced out to get them wet again.

Where Mary Lee stood, the ice on the lake was not solidly frozen. A little brook kept it mushy. Little orange signs on thin metal rods said over and over THIN ICE, THIN ICE, THIN ICE.

Jon Pear held her from behind, his arms encircling her.

The day grew colder, the sky thinner, its blue watered down with winter chill. People stood closer and shivered, and made fists of their fingers inside their mittens. People curled their toes inside their boots and tucked their hands beneath their arms.

"Where does the relay team skate?" asked Jon Pear.

"Way over there," said Mary Lee. "The ice is three full inches thick over there."

"But over here," said Jon Pear, as if he had discovered treasure, "it isn't."

Her mother and father were laughing with the other parents. Judges and PTA officers, teachers, and older brothers and sisters home from college, were everywhere. She took a step toward the crowd she yearned for: Van and Scarlett, Kip, Geordie and Courtney.

Jon Pear did not move. His weight kept her tethered. "This is a good vantage point," remarked Jon Pear. "If anything goes wrong, we'll have a good view." Jon Pear was enjoying himself. If she fought against his grip, he'd enjoy it more. If she didn't fight, he'd win.

Sweet, innocent, brightly clad children, thinking only of snow and ribbons, ice and prizes, swarmed and danced, skated and raced.

The crowd of her classmates suddenly surged toward Mary Lee and Jon Pear. How grim their expressions were. How determined they looked.

They were coming for revenge.

Would they include Mary Lee in it? Would they make her pay for Madrigal's deeds? Did they even believe that she was Mary Lee?

Mary Lee tried a third time to step free of Jon Pear and, as she leaned and struggled, he released her so suddenly she fell onto the hard ground and cried out in pain.

Jon Pear smiled.

Van lifted her up.

Scarlett moved between her and Jon Pear.

And the students surrounded Jon Pear.

Home-grown justice, thought Mary Lee. They have come to do away with Jon Pear.

The boys were armed. Not with knives, not with guns, not with stones. They carried icicles. Long vicious sharp icicles. Nothing would melt in this weather. And icicles would penetrate a heart as well as steel.

"No," whispered Mary Lee.

"Yes," said the crowd. They surrounded Jon Pear. He merely continued to smile, his expression filled with superior loathing.

The crowd hated that smile. They would wipe it off.

"It's time, Jon Pear," said Van. "You're going to get yours."

Jon Pear raised his eyebrows skeptically.

"You pride yourself on standing by and watching people suffer," said Katy. "We're going to see how that feels. Because we're going to stand by and watch *you* suffer."

Jon Pear laughed.

"We won't actually do anything to you," added Courtney. "We'll be passive."

"I think," said Geordie, "that he should drown the way he and Madrigal watched that man drown." Armed with ice, Geordie hardly looked passive. He looked truly and willingly violent.

A flicker crossed Jon Pear's face. He was not so sure of this situation after all.

"I vote to have Jon Pear drown," said Katy.

Jon Pear was taller and broader than most, and he gazed around, casually, as if bored. But he saw no way out, and he was not bored.

"Second," said Van.

"All in favor?" said Katy.

"Aye," chorused the students.

"All opposed?" said Katy, and they laughed because nobody would be opposed to the end of Jon Pear.

"I'm opposed," said Mary Lee. Her voice hung like spun sugar in the freezing air.

They stepped away from Mary Lee, and Mary Lee stepped away from them, and even further from Jon Pear. "It isn't right," she said. "You have to give people what you would like them to give you." She swallowed. "We have to be decent, whether Jon Pear is or not."

Jon Pear's laugh flipped in wild peals like a Frisbee.

"Listen to him!" shouted Van. "He knows you're nothing but a patsy, saying he should go free! Does he have you in his spell the way he had Madrigal? There has to be an end to people like Jon Pear! Let him drown."

The group agreed, chorus-like, singing and swaying along.

They pressed forward, and Jon Pear was forced back a step, and then two steps, and then the heel of his boot was in the mush and sliding down.

"No!" said Mary Lee. "We can't."

"Watch us," said Courtney.

They were a mob, and they were going on without her.

She had not stopped her twin, she had not stopped Jon Pear, she could not stop this mob. She had no silver tongue and had convinced nobody of anything.

On Jon Pear's face, a tear of panic formed. He swung wildly, looking for a way out, and the tear was flung out over the ice and replaced by another tear.

"He's scared!" said Katy. "Oh, good! He's scared!"

Across the lake, a little skater left the course.

Head down, feet pumping, the small bright-blue-clad racer was thinking only of speed. The shouts from the crowd, shouts of his name — *Bryan! Bryan!* — meant nothing; Bryan thought they were his fans.

His legs were short and, even on skates, his strides were short.

The judge abandoned his position at the end of the race course and ran — not on skates, but on slippery rubber boots — to stop Bryan.

Parents left the shore, and shouting, skidding, falling, tried to stop Bryan.

The little boy flew across the last of the solid ice, and vanished as quick as a stone through the possessive mush of the bad ice.

Jon Pear was closest.

"Save him!" shrieked Mary Lee. "Jon Pear! Go out after him!"

But Jon Pear had only himself on his mind, and the mob had only Jon Pear. Mary Lee ran out on the ice, passing them, screaming, "Jon Pear! Do something good for a change!"

She too wore no skates, and her rubber soles slipped. But she knew this lake. It was shallow at this end. If she fell through, she was tall enough to stand. She just had to get to Bryan, yank him up, pull him out of the water that would stop his heart.

She fell through the ice yards from where Bryan had gone down. She righted herself, smashing the ice between them with her fists. The cold was so bad, it was like being burned. She felt as if her legs would be amputated by the water itself.

On the shore, the teenagers abandoned Jon Pear and flung themselves through the ice, to help from their side.

But they were too far and too late.

Mary Lee waded forward somehow, making herself an icebreaker, using muscles she had not possessed when she was fighting Jon Pear.

The bright bright blue of Bryan's jacket showed through the cold cold water.

Mary Lee pulled him up, dragging him out of the water, holding him high. Geordie and Van reached her, and the teenagers passed the little boy from arm to arm, a bucket brigade, handing him at last to the parents on dry land.

* * *

When the ambulance had arrived, and Bryan was breathing and yelling that he didn't want to go to the hospital, he still wanted to be in his race, they relaxed.

Relaxed enough to remember who and where they were.

And Katy said, "Where's Jon Pear?"

Nobody still held an icicle. Nobody still formed a mob. They were just kids, thrilled to have saved a life, proud of themselves, and very very wet and cold.

Jon Pear was nowhere. They stared across the churned and broken ice at the long expanse of frozen lake where the skating had begun again.

"Maybe he was supernatural," whispered Katy. "Maybe he dematerialized."

Mary Lee knew better. But she didn't know where Jon Pear was. Where could he have gone? How did he get there without anybody noticing?

"Come on, Mary Lee," said Scarlet, "I brought a change of clothing. You'll have to put it on — quick — before you die of exposure."

Mary Lee still looked for Jon Pear. He wasn't the kind of person you wanted to lose track of. You didn't want him at your back.

"Mary Lee, your ski suit's turning to ice right on your body," said Scarlett. "Move it."

But when she moved it, she saw the colors in the water. Bright bleeding colors. Beneath the churned ice. Floating in the frigid water.

She stepped forward, to see more clearly, and Geordie and Kip, Kenneth and Stephen, stepped between her and the ice.

"It'll freeze over again," said Geordie.

"Temperature's dropping as we speak," said Kip.

"Time to go in," said Van.

This mob. Her new friends. Had they held him under? Had they trampled him when she thought they were rushing to rescue Bryan? Or had Jon Pear slipped of his own accord, and just as *he* never rescued anybody, nobody rescued him?

Which of these boys and girls had shrugged and let him drown? Or had he let himself drown? Had he known, for a few seconds at least, how evil he was?

I will never know what Madrigal really planned to do on that visit, she thought. I will never know why she switched ski suits with me, or what would have happened if the ski lift hadn't broken.

And unless I ask, I will never know how Jon Pear found his way beneath the ice, to stay there until spring.

"Carry her," advised Katy. "I think she's

going into shock herself. Lift her up on your shoulders and carry her to the warming cabin."

They were ready to let the ice freeze over, and the past stay past.

They lifted her up and ran, a bunch of boys holding a pretty girl in the air. She jounced in the aching cold, held up by the flat palms of nice young men, who had taken justice into those same hands. People shouted and cheered, thinking she was the princess of Winter Sleigh Day. Thinking there must have been a vote they didn't know about.

There was a vote, thought Mary Lee. And I voted no. I have to remember that. I wasn't able to stop evil, but I didn't stand and watch it, either. Jon Pear didn't win. I won.

I'm Mary Lee. And I'm glad.

About the Author

Caroline B. Cooney lives in a small seacoast village in Connecticut. She writes every day on a word processor and then goes for a long walk down to the beach to figure out what she's going to write the following day. She's written fifty books for young people; including *The Cheerleader*, *The Return of the Vampire* and the *Vampire's Promise*. Her other thrillers include *The Perfume, Freeze Tag* and *The Stranger*. She reads as much as possible, and she has three grown children.

Point Horror Unleashed

Point Horror Unleashed.
It's one step beyond...